RED ROSE GIRL

District Nurse Sophie Draycott loved her job and the patients she visited, but she was beginning to feel that her boyfriend, Robert Williams, was too serious and boring. He was also taking her too much for granted. Then into her life came Brett Ridgeway, the grandson of one of her elderly patients. Sophie was sure she knew which of the two men had captured her heart, but she had no control over the way fate helped her to be absolutely certain.

KAREN ABBOTT

RED ROSE GIRL

Complete and Unabridged

LINFORD
Leicester

ASK— 2777 S/02

First published in Great Britain

First Linford Edition
published 2002

British Library CIP Data

Abbott, Karen
    Red rose girl.—Large print ed.—
Linford romance library
    1. Love stories
    2. Large type books
    I. Title
    823.9'14 [F]

ISBN 0–7089–9812–7

Published by
F. A. Thorpe (Publishing)
Anstey, Leicestershire

Set by Words & Graphics Ltd.
Anstey, Leicestershire
Printed and bound in Great Britain by
T. J. International Ltd., Padstow, Cornwall

This book is printed on acid-free paper

1

Don't be silly! District nurses don't normally drive around in trendy MG sports cars!'

Recalling Robert Williams' reaction to her not-too-serious suggestion, a grin split across Sophie Draycott's face as she crossed the health centre carpark to where her electric-blue, seen-better-days Ford Fiesta was parked. Dropping her medical bag on to the rear seat, she got into the driving seat.

She hadn't really meant it, about the MG, but Robert's reaction was changing her mind. What else had he said? Far too trendy? She'd show him! Her grin faded. Trendy certainly wasn't the adjective anyone would apply to Robert! Serious, even boring was what sprang more readily to mind, and, for some unknown reason, that suddenly seemed irksome to her. She didn't want to be tied to someone who was serious or boring. She needed some light relief in her life, some spontaneous laughter, something to replace the frown that she knew was furrowing her face.

She turned the ignition key and grimaced as the engine made a feeble effort to start. Robert was taking far too many things for granted, such as his priority to her free time. Her other friends didn't call quite so often. In fact, just when had someone last suggested she went out with them? She couldn't recall.

The cool April air had put a pink blush on her cheeks and a restless spring in her heart. Maybe it was time she moved on. She turned the ignition key again and the engine burst into life.

All thoughts of Robert slipped out of her mind as she began her rounds and, for the next few hours, she was fully occupied in dealing with a long list of home visits. Charlotte Turner, seven and a half months pregnant with her first baby, was obediently resting as much as she could and was keeping the fluid retention under control. Tom Cluney's boils were healing nicely and a few drops in Mark Dobson's infected ear sorted him out for the day.

Concern marked her face as she left elderly Mrs Carter's cottage. Those ulcers weren't healing as they should and her leg was quite a mess, but the mention of hospital had sent the elderly lady into a burst of adamant refusals. Sophie made a few notes in her diary and turned her thoughts to her next home visit, dressing Mrs Millfield's burns following a frying pan accident, and quite nasty burns they were, too.

Her working life was certainly full of variety, she mused. Maybe that was why she had dallied so long over telling Robert that it was time for a change. He was solid and dependable and would probably be exactly the same in thirty or forty years' time. It was time to go their separate ways, but not tonight. She was partnering him to an important social evening tomorrow and didn't want to leave him in the lurch.

Her flat on the edge of town overlooked the road that led up to the local high school, nestling against the most southerly end of the Pennines, where they came tumbling down to meet the West Lancashire Plain. By the time she arrived home, the stream of buses, cars, bicycles and groups of chattering school children had long passed by and all was quiet again. She put on the kettle and kicked off her shoes. A long soak in the bath seemed a good idea, and then an evening with Robert.

She knew exactly where they would go and where they would be sitting. On Friday nights it was the corner table in The Jolly Crofter's. He would order soup of the day for his starter, a medium-rare steak with chips and side salad for main course, and finish with cheese and biscuits. A carafe of red house-wine would accompany the steak. Sophie sighed. If only he would go mad once in a while and have something different.

Her fragrant hot bath was marred by recurring thoughts of Mrs Carter's ulcers. An image of their inflamed state flashed in front of her eyes. She hoped they weren't going septic. The last thing the old lady needed was blood poisoning. Maybe Robert wouldn't mind if she popped in to see her again on their way out.

'Isn't that rather overdoing it?' Robert asked tartly, when she put the proposition to him. 'I wouldn't have thought the money you get warrants such dedication.'

Sophie turned to pick up her bag.

'If I was in it for the money, I'd be in the wrong job,' she said quietly. 'Mrs Carter is an elderly lady who lives on her own, and she's in pain. I feel concerned and I'd rather not leave it until tomorrow. However, if you don't wish to come with me . . . '

Robert looked at his watch.

'Our table is booked for eight o'clock. There's not really time.'

Sophie sighed.

'OK. Then I'll take my own car and join you later. She lives down Alexandra Road. I shouldn't be too long.'

His expression became thoughtful.

'Well, it's not that far out of the way, is it? Go on, I'll take you. Never let it be said that I don't spoil you.'

He leaned over and dropped a surprise kiss on her lips.

'It'll give me a chance to see you in action. Sample your bedside manner and all that.'

His jocular tones made her blink in amazement, but Robert was already holding out her coat for her to slip her arms into.

'Well, thank you, if you're sure you don't mind.'

She carefully locked the door and followed Robert down the stairs. Well, miracles would never cease! Robert had actually been light-hearted. Maybe she shouldn't be too ready to move on. There was hope yet. His happy mood continued on the short journey to Mrs Carter's home, where she lived alone, with only her cat, Blackie, for company. It was a stone-built cottage, its garden full of flowers and a small, neat lawn.

'Our Brett does it for me,' Mrs Carter frequently told Sophie.

Sophie was pleased that her grandson conscientiously visited and helped her so much. Her job would be all the harder without family help and care.

Robert parked the car and was around at her side, holding open the door before she had time to gather herself together.

'Your destination, madame,' he quipped.

'Thank you, Williams,' she replied in similar tone.

Then she returned her voice to normal.

'Are you coming in? Or do you want to stay here? It's a bit cramped in there.'

Robert didn't answer immediately. He ran his practised eye over the old building.

'Hmm, I bet this place is cold in

winter time,' he ventured. 'And a few slates look a bit dodgy up there.'

'Robert! Will you leave your county surveyor's hat at home, please?' Sophie cautioned. 'I don't want Mrs Carter being upset about the state of her home. She has enough to deal with over the state of her legs.'

Robert grasped her elbow, as they walked up the path.

'I may as well come in with you, now that I'm here. You never know, a different face might cheer the old dear up a bit.'

Sophie knocked on the door, then bent down to push open the letter-box flap.

'It's only me, Mrs Carter, Sister Draycott. I've come to see your legs again.'

She turned to look up at Robert.

'She's coming.'

She straightened up and watched through the small, bevelled-glass panel as the indistinct shape of an elderly woman hobbled towards the front door.

The safety chain rattled and the door opened.

'I wasn't expecting you again, Sister Draycott. You should be out enjoying yourself on a Friday night, not visiting an old woman like me.'

She opened the door wide as she spoke, painfully moving backwards a few paces.

'Come on in. Oh, and this is your young man? Eeh, you look lovely with your hair down, Sister. You're a lucky young man,' she added, wagging her finger at Robert.

Sophie bent her head slightly and stepped inside. As they stepped straight into the front room, Robert's eyes roved expertly over the small, dark patches above the bay-window frame. She nudged him in exasperation. Didn't he ever take time off work?

The room was pleasant and homely-looking, though a bit on the dark side, due to the small bay-window, where a pair of red and white gingham curtains hung. A vase of imitation red poppies sat on the window ledge. A low fire burned in the grate. Various ornaments decorated the many wooden surfaces, sitting in a liberal coating of dust, Sophie couldn't help noticing. Mrs Carter followed her glance.

'I've not done me dusting today, love. It's me legs, you know. They're not what they were.'

'That's all right, Mrs Carter. I haven't done mine either. Now, why don't you sit down in your chair and I'll take another look at those ulcers? I hope you don't mind me bringing Robert with me.'

'No, I like to see plenty of young folk. Does me good, you know. Nice to see you, Robert.'

Robert charmed her with a smile. 'Pleased to meet you, Mrs Carter. What an interesting home you have. Do you own it?'

Sophie turned her attention to the ulcers. She wasn't at all happy about them. She wondered if she ought to get one of the practice doctors to pop in and see them. She must make a note of it in her diary for tomorrow. She carefully changed the dressing, casually mentioning her concern. Mrs Carter reacted immediately.

'I don't want none of them young doctors poking about me. I'd much rather leave it to you, Sister Draycott. Happen they'll be fine by morning. You'll see.'

Sophie sat back on her heels.

'I'll tell you what,' she conceded. 'I'll see how they are tomorrow, but, if I'm still not happy, then I really will have to get a doctor to see to them. All right?'

'Right you are, love,' Mrs Carter replied with a smile.

Robert was looking up at a hair-line crack in the ceiling. Sophie touched his arm.

'Come on, Robert. I've finished. It's time to go.'

She turned back to Mrs Carter.

'See you tomorrow, then. No, don't get up. We'll see ourselves out. 'Bye, 'bye.'

Robert drove silently for a while, his face serious. Sophie was touched that he shared her concern for her elderly patient.

'I hope I can keep her at home,' she eventually commented. 'She has such a dread of going into hospital. Her late husband was taken in after a fall, and he died a week later. She thinks the same will happen to her.'

'What?' Robert's voice was startled. 'Oh, yes. I see what you mean, poor soul. Has she any family?'

'She mentions a grandson, so I suppose she must have a son or daughter somewhere around. I don't know them. They aren't on our lists, so they either live farther away or go to a different surgery. Why do you ask?'

'Oh, no reason, just curious. It must be sad to be alone. I think you should keep an eye on her, let her know she has a friend.'

Sophie was again touched by his concern. She looked at him in a new light. She had greatly underestimated him, it seemed.

Saturday was another busy day. Sophie's schedule was already planned, so it wasn't until it was going on for half-past five that she was able to squeeze in the extra visit to Mrs Carter. She rang the bell and called through the letter-box.

'Hello? Mrs Carter? It's Sister Draycott to see you.'

There was no response, so she called again. She listened carefully. She was sure she wouldn't have gone out anywhere, not with those bad legs of hers. Unless someone had taken her out? She listened again. She couldn't be sure, but she thought she heard a faint sound.

'Mrs Carter! It's me, Sister Draycott. Are you all right?'

This time, she was sure of it. Mrs Carter was there, but something was preventing her coming to the door. A quick glance at the front window showed that there was no chance of getting in there, and the door was fastened too securely to be pushed in. Even the bevelled-glass centre panel was too thick to break easily and she doubted she could reach the catch through it, anyway. She had better try round the back.

She raced around the side of the cottage. Now, that looked hopeful. The kitchen window was partly open. It was almost shoulder height but an old, disused mangle, covered with a number of trailing pot-plants, only needed to be dragged across the stone flags to give her a handy leg-up. She balanced her bag on the top and hitched her skirt up above her knees. The cottage backed on to fields. She hoped no-one was watching as she scrambled up on to the mangle.

She glanced over her shoulder. One of the plants wobbled and fell with a crash, then another. Not to worry! They could be replaced. She struggled to her feet, grabbing hold of the window-frame to haul herself up farther. The mangle wobbled precariously. She held her breath, waiting until she felt steady again. The next bit might be tricky. She had to keep her balance, whilst she unhooked the window clasp and pulled the window out towards her. She managed it.

'I'm coming, Mrs Carter,' she called through the window. 'Hang on! I won't be long. I've just to put my bag inside.'

The window was over the sink. She was relieved to see that the washing-up bowl was empty. Now, if she could just move the dishes and plates off the draining-board into the bowl, her way in would be clear. There!

She would have preferred to have gone in feet first, but there wasn't room to manoeuvre on the rickety mangle, so, head first it had to be, hoping that she would be able to turn round on the draining-board, otherwise it was going to be a painful slither down to the kitchen floor. She hitched up her skirt once more. Here goes!

As she ducked her head in through the window, she screamed. A hand had grabbed her ankle and an angry male voice called out, 'Oh, no, you don't!'

2

Sophie screamed again. Her flailing hand sent her bag flying off the draining-board and her head banged against the window frame. The strong hands pulled her backwards over the window-sill, where the grip was swiftly moved to around her waist, before swinging her bodily through the air and dumping her unceremoniously upon her feet.

'Got you!'

'Just what do you think you are doing?' Sophie shouted angrily at exactly the same moment.

The two regarded each other in fury.

Sophie stepped back, her eyes making a quick appraisal of the man who was towering over her. She was acutely aware that her hat had been knocked off her head and her mass of shoulder-length hair had tumbled out of the neat chignon she preferred when working.

The man was extremely good-looking, especially now that the angry glare in his dark brown eyes was fading into a bemused uncertainty, as he took in the crumpled lines of her district nurse's uniform. He seemed to be a pleasant young man, a man to be trusted, she guessed instinctively. His very presence caused a flow of excitement to ripple around her body, but there was no way she was going to show it right now!

She drew herself up to her full five feet nine inches, which was just about level with the knot of his tie.

'I don't know who you are,' she said, trying to smooth down her uniform and regain some of her lost dignity, 'or what you think I was up to, but there's an old lady in there who might be in need of assistance and I would be obliged if you would help me to get back through that window so that I can see what is the matter.'

The man smiled ruefully, his strong, wide mouth revealing his perfect white teeth, though the twinkle in his eyes showed that he wasn't entirely repentant over what he had just done.

'I thought you were breaking in, but . . . er . . . wouldn't it have been easier to go through the door?'

Sophie watched in open-mouthed dismay as he reached past her and twisted the knob on the back door. She wished the ground would open to swallow her up as it swung open.

'Gran knew I was coming, and she left the door unlocked for me,' he was saying.

Gran? He was Mrs Carter's grandson?

'You can't be! Mrs Carter's grandson is a Boy Scout. You're far too old!'

He grinned impishly, making the three-fingered salute.

'Scout Master Brett Ridgeway at your service, ma'am.'

He looked as if he was enjoying her embarrassment.

'And you? You must be the wonderful Sister Draycott Gran talks about. Delighted to meet you. Come on in.'

Sophie knew she was gaping at him in a most unladylike way. His disarming smile went some way to smoothing her ruffled feathers. There was no doubt that he was a very handsome, young man and, if the light in his dark brown eyes was anything to go by, he didn't exactly think that she was a plain Jane.

The thought made her heart warm within her and sent a tingle of joyful anticipation rippling down her spine.

However, enough of this! She was on duty and Mrs Carter still wasn't accounted for. She swung her head away from him and stepped briskly into the kitchen, pausing only to pick up her fallen bag.

'Oh, no!'

Immediately, she rushed towards the inner door to the front room, where she had already spotted part of the old lady's fallen figure. Mrs Carter was barely conscious, though she did seem to be aware that help had come. Her right foot was twisted under her at an unusual angle and Sophie was almost sure that it was broken.

'Go upstairs for some blankets,' she ordered Brett.

She swiftly made a preliminary examination of the old lady.

'I don't know how long she's been here like this, but she seems pretty cold. I'll phone for an ambulance.'

That done, she dropped back down again beside Mrs Carter, gently chaffing her hands to get her blood flowing a little better.

'You'll be all right now, Mrs Carter. We'll soon have you sorted out,' she said gently.

Mrs Carter groaned and stirred restlessly. Brett was already back at her side, the blankets in his hands.

Whilst he was wrapping them around his grandmother, Sophie noticed Brett carefully placing Mrs Carter's head to one side on the slim pillow he had also brought downstairs with him.

'Is that better, Gran?'

His voice was warm and gentle, and at the sound of his voice, Mrs Carter slowly opened her eyes and managed a brief, if twisted, smile. Her face perked up somewhat as she recognised her rescuers.

'Brett, dear, and Sister Draycott. Thank goodness! I'm a silly old woman, aren't I?'

'Less of the old,' Brett teased, leaning over to plant a kiss on her cheek. 'What were you up to?'

'I tripped over Blackie on the way down stairs. I couldn't stop myself. Eeh, I hope he's all right. He shot out through the window.'

Sophie smiled reassuringly at the old lady.

'Don't worry, he'll be back when he's hungry.'

'What's going to happen to me?' Mrs Carter said worriedly. 'I can't even stand up.'

She tried to struggle into a sitting position but Brett was quick to gently hold her down.

'I don't have to go to hospital, do I, Sister? What would happen to Blackie? I'd much rather stay here. I'm sure I'll manage, once I'm up on my feet!'

Sophie patted her hand.

'I'm sorry, Mrs Carter, but I'm not happy about your ankle. Hospital really is the better option. But, don't worry! I'll come with you, and Brett will, too, I'm sure.'

She turned to look enquiringly at him. Brett nodded.

'Yes, of course, and don't worry about Blackie. We'll think of something.'

Brett squeezed her hand.

'The main thing is that you're made all right again.'

★ ★ ★

Between them, they managed to keep up a steady stream of light chatter to keep Mrs Carter as cheerful as possible whilst they waited for the ambulance to arrive.

As Brett recounted an amusing camp-fire tale, Sophie stole a look at his face. It was kind and full of caring. The tiny crinkles around his eyes added to the warmth of his smile. She felt relaxed in his company, as they cheerfully chatted, keeping Mrs Carter alert but relaxed. They seemed to share common interests and laugh at the same sort of jokes. He was nice, she decided, wondering if he had any romantic attachments, and hoping he didn't!

Eventually, the ambulance came and the medics transferred Mrs Carter to a stretcher. Sophie elected to travel with her patient, leaving Brett to follow in his car.

As soon as she could leave Mrs Carter for a moment, she phoned the health centre answering service to report what had happened and then rang Robert to explain her delay at arriving home. She was shocked to realise what time it was. Where had it gone to? She knew that she would have to rush if she were to have time to shower and change.

Robert hated to be even a minute late for anything, especially an event such as this, that was sponsored by one of the local political parties, of which Robert was a keen member. It would be the sort of evening that everyone stood around for hours, sipping cocktails and making trite, political observations.

It wasn't her idea of a congenial night out but Robert liked to have a pretty girl on his arm on these occasions.

Robert's voice, when she finally got through, was extremely curt. She was left in no doubt as to what he thought about her careless lack of timing.

'It's most inconsiderate of you, Sophie. I am disappointed in you. You know how important these occasions are to the furtherance of my career! Don't bother yourself to rush home! I shall have to find a replacement, though at this late hour, I really don't know who.'

He rang off before she had time to

apologise again. She grimaced at the phone in her hand. Trust Robert to be so snooty and high-handed! As she replaced the receiver on to its rest, she felt slightly guilty to find herself so little perturbed by his reaction to her last-minute defection, but she was quite sure he would quickly find someone else to drape on his arm in her absence.

Brett had followed the ambulance in his own car. By the time he had parked and made his way to the Accident and Emergency Department, Sophie was just returning.

'How bad is she?' he asked.

'Her ankle is broken. She's been taken to X-ray to confirm it but I think it's a foregone conclusion. There is quite a bit of bruising, which will get worse before it gets better. I pointed out the ulcers that aren't healing properly and they are all agreed that she needs to be admitted, as soon as a bed can be found for her. She'll need her ankle to be set first, of course, which means a general anaesthetic, I'm afraid. But they promised to get it done as soon as they can. At your grandmother's age, one of the main concerns is the shock to her system.'

She was leading the way through the busy department whilst she was talking, where they found Mrs Carter back in the cubicle, slightly propped up and revived enough for her to be able to hold out her hands.

'I'm a nuisance, aren't I? But I am glad you stayed, Sister. You've been company for Brett, too. I told you he was a lovely boy, didn't I?' she said.

Sophie grinned at his embarrassment. 'You certainly did!'

'Anyway, I won't be long now. The nurse said the doctor's on his way, so I'll be able to get home to Blackie. He hasn't been fed yet, you know. He'll be hungry.'

Sophie and Brett exchanged glances.

It was Brett who took the plunge and told her that she would be staying in hospital for a while.

'But I can't. What'll happen to

Blackie? I must go home. He'll fret too much without me!'

She began to struggle to get off the trolley as she spoke. Brett gently took hold of her hand.

'Gran, your ankle is broken, so you won't be able to get around properly for a while, and you've got those ulcers on your leg. There's no way you can be left alone to take care of yourself at the moment. Isn't that right, Sister?'

Sophie nodded.

'Yes, and don't worry. I'll look after Blackie for you, Mrs Carter. I can pop in and feed him on my way to and from work or if I'm out on a call that way. He often stays out at nights, doesn't he? I'll put a box and a blanket for him in that old shed round the back.'

'And I'll keep popping over to keep an eye on the place,' Brett assured her. 'I might be able to keep an eye on Sister Draycott at the same time,' he added with a cheeky grin.

He then smiled engagingly at Sophie.

She blushed prettily, thinking that she would quite enjoy Brett looking after her, but she tilted her nose cheekily into the air.

'I can look after myself, thank you,' she retorted, with mock indignation. 'But, seriously speaking, don't you worry, Mrs Carter. We'll take care of everything for you. And we'll have a royal welcome awaiting you when you come home.'

'I will come home, won't I?'

Sophie squeezed her hand.

'Of course, you will. Don't you worry.'

Reluctant to leave until Mrs Carter was comfortably settled in the orthopaedic ward, it was after nine o'clock when at last Sophie and Brett felt free to leave her.

'I don't know about you, but I'm hungry,' Brett commented, looking at his watch. 'Do you fancy a quick bite somewhere? Unless you have other plans, of course.'

'No, nothing important but I'm still

29

in uniform. I can't really go out dressed like this.'

She was truly regretful, she realised.

'And my hair! Heavens! I must look a mess!'

She hastily tucked a few stray tendrils behind her ear. Brett smiled.

'Not at all!' he assured her. 'But, I tell you what. Why don't we pick up a take-away from somewhere, call back at Gran's cottage to make sure that everything is all right there and feed Blackie and then I'll accompany you home, to make sure you get there all right? You've had a long day.'

That was agreed.

They bought two Chinese take-aways, which they ate in Mrs Carter's front room, with Blackie sitting between them on the fireside rug, contentedly washing his paws, after a tasty, if late, cat-food dinner.

They spent a couple of humour-filled hours, which were over all too quickly.

By the time Sophie waved Brett goodbye from her front door, she realised that she had spent the happiest Saturday evening for more months than she cared to remember, yet they had done nothing special.

It must be the company, she reflected, feeling slightly guilty because she had let Robert down and had had a good evening, herself, in spite of that.

There was a curt message from Robert on her answer machine, obviously left there before her call to him, voicing his displeasure at her absence and wanting to know what she was playing at. It rather took the shine off the evening, but the memory of Brett Ridgeway's smile and the tingle that the touch of his hand had sent running down her spine brought a smile to the corners of her mouth and she couldn't help hoping that he would get in touch with her again.

3

Sophie tried to phone Robert as soon as she returned home from church on Sunday morning, wanting to clear the air between them, but there was no answer. She left a message on his answer machine and turned away to flick on the TV whilst she made herself some lunch.

The phone rang. She picked up the receiver.

'Robert?'

'Sorry to disappoint you,' she heard Brett's voice apologise.

Her heart began to beat quickly.

'Oh, Brett! I'm not disappointed,' she assured him. 'It's just that I've been trying to get in touch with . . . er . . . a friend, to explain about last night. Remember, I told you I should have been at a PR event. I just wanted to apologise again for letting him down.'

'And I wanted to thank you for being so kind to my gran,' Brett continued.

Had his voice lost some of its warmth? She wasn't sure. Did he think she was going behind Robert's back?

'That's all right,' she replied non-committally. 'I would do the same for any patient under the same circumstances.'

'Yes, I think you would,' he agreed. 'I noticed you had also been to feed Blackie at some time this morning. I must have just missed you. What I wondered was,' he went on, his voice warming, but still hesitant, 'would you care to make a follow-up visit to your patient this afternoon, maybe after a nice lunch somewhere? That is, if you've nothing else planned.'

'That sounds lovely. So, yes, I would. Where are you now?'

'At Gran's cottage. I can be with you in about ten minutes. That all right? Please just say if it's not convenient,' he added tentatively.

'That's just great, honestly. See you soon.'

She swiftly changed into a pair of casual trousers and light top, with a sweater draped casually over her shoulders. She brushed her long golden hair into light, loose waves and applied a light touch of lipstick. When the doorbell rang, she just had to pick up her small shoulder bag and run lightly down the stairs. She opened the door.

'Oh!' she exclaimed — it was Robert, and she knew a guilty flush had covered her cheeks. 'Robert! I didn't expect you.'

'Obviously not! Whom did you expect? It wouldn't be whoever it was you ditched me for last night, would it?'

'It wasn't like that,' she protested. 'I told you. My elderly patient, Mrs Carter, you remember, actually needed to be taken to hospital.'

'Oh!'

He paused for a moment.

'Do you mean her cottage is left empty? Do you think she'll ever go back to it? Old property deteriorates if it's left empty for too long.'

'I don't know. She hopes to return home but it's too soon to say. Anyway, after your show of concern on Friday evening, I thought you would understand.'

'Yes, well, I must say I thought you were uncharacteristically inconsiderate towards me. You could have helped me to make a very good impression on the selection committee last night. As it was, I had to make do with Joanna Parker.'

He suddenly broke off, as he noticed what she was wearing. A look of distaste flickered across his face.

'I've told you before that I don't like you in trousers, Sophie. You'll have to change, of course. I thought we might just make it for lunch at the golf club. One or two of the committee happened to mention that they would be there today. I've reserved a table for us. Run upstairs and put a pretty dress on, there's a good girl!'

Sophie gritted her teeth.

'I have apologised for last night,

Robert, and I'm going out for lunch with someone else. It's already arranged.'

She looked anxiously up and down the road, hoping that Brett wouldn't arrive just yet. Robert didn't miss out on her anxiety.

'It's another man, isn't it?'

Sophie met his eyes unwaveringly.

'Yes, it is, and he'll be here soon. So I'd appreciate it if . . . '

'And how long has this been going on?'

'Nothing has been going on. We only met last night. He's Mrs Carter's grandson. We are going to have lunch and then go to visit her in hospital.'

He shook his head sadly.

'I really am disappointed in you, Sophie. I thought we had a better understanding than this. However, I'm sure we can come to some compromise. He's probably just being a little too over-conscientious in his gratitude towards you. I'm sure he won't object if you change your mind. In fact, I'll wait here to tell him so, whilst you go up to change.'

He smiled with satisfaction at his solution, but Sophie stood her ground.

'I'm sorry, Robert, but I am lunching with Brett. You and I hadn't made plans to meet.'

'You know I expect you to come to these special lunches with me. You might have checked with me first.'

He sounded extremely aggrieved.

'You expect too much, Robert. You don't own me. I'm sorry if I've upset you. I didn't mean to. Now, if you don't mind . . .'

Robert's lips tightened as he took in what she was saying.

'I am not upset. On the contrary, my dear, I think it's as well I've learned how unreliable you are, before wasting any more of my time on you. Goodbye!'

Without a further word, he swung around, got into his car and drove off at speed. Sophie watched him drive off. She hated confrontational scenes and was sorry to have been the cause of this one, but it had to happen sometime. Even so, it left her feeling she could have handled it better.

She was glad when Brett arrived. His cheerful chatter soon pushed away Robert's departure from her life. In fact, she felt as if a grey cloud had been lifted. It was a beautiful, late-spring day, a day for enjoyment, laughter, a day for ... her heart skipped a beat ... for lovers!

'You look gorgeous,' Brett complimented her when he greeted her. 'I love your hair down like that.'

He reached out a hand and touched it lightly.

'It ripples like a field of corn.'

Sophie felt a warm shiver down her back.

'Flatterer!' she teased.

She was a little unused to compliments of late but found she liked it. The look in Brett's eyes told her that he meant it.

'It's such a lovely day, I've got the top down on the car,' he went on. 'Do you mind?'

'No. I thought you might. I'm looking forward to it. I'll put my sweater on. Here, hold this.'

She handed him her bag and swiftly dragged the sweater over her head. He reached out and helped to free some of her hair that was caught inside the neckline, his fingers brushing the nape of her neck. She delighted at his touch. It had that magical, magnetic thrill, like an electric current, that made her want to sway into it. However, she contented herself with a dazzling smile, matched by his own.

'I'm ready! Let's go!' he said, switching on the ignition.

She loved it. She closed her eyes and lifted her face up to the warmth of the sun's rays, delighting to feel the breeze blowing back her hair. They were driving along Chorley Old Road, almost on the edge of the moors. Sophie sensed Brett glance at her. She opened her eyes and smiled at him.

'Oh, this is lovely!'

'Yes. I like it up here. It reminds me of home.'

'Oh, and where is that?'

'Well,' he teased, smiling down at her, 'let's say, in the Wars of the Roses, I'd have worn the wrong colour of rose for you.'

'What? Oh! A Yorkshire man! Well, I can cope with that! What is it they say? Yorkshire born and Yorkshire bred, strong in the arm and weak in the head?'

Brett threw back his head and laughed.

'That's funny! We learned it as Lancashire born and Lancashire bred!'

His dancing eyes flung out a challenge, as they flicked from the road to her and back again. Sophie responded with a delighted grin.

'I notice you left Yorkshire and came to live in Lancashire!'

'Ah, yes! That's because I thought your red roses needed a bit of help!'

'Came to learn from us, more like!'

They grinned briefly at each other,

before Brett turned his attention back to the road. Sophie settled back against her seat in contentment. She was enjoying the banter between them. She suddenly felt liberated, free to be herself.

After a very nice lunch at an old coaching inn, and a stroll around the grounds, fingers linked with each other, they visited Mrs Carter, pleased to find her sitting propped up against some pillows and full of information about the other patients in the ward.

'You sound as though you're enjoying this,' Brett teased her. 'It isn't supposed to be a holiday camp, you know!'

'Get away with you! Me in a holiday camp! I'll be up and pushing that trolley around before long!'

Brett laughed.

'I don't doubt it!'

They stayed until they sensed that Mrs Carter was in need of a rest, making assurances that Blackie and the cottage were in good hands while she was away. They had agreed that Sophie would take responsibility for Blackie's morning feeds and Brett would take care of him in the evenings. Sophie now wondered what Brett had in mind for the remainder of the day. Her reports were up to date and she didn't really fancy spending the rest of the day on her own. She needn't have worried.

'Have you ever done any line dancing?' Brett asked, as they left the hospital.

'No, but I've often thought I would like to try. Have you?'

'Yes. I go most Wednesday nights, but there's an extra one tonight. It's a charity night, with a hot-pot supper. Do you fancy giving it a go?'

'It sounds fun.'

'Good. Why don't we buy a pint of milk and something light to eat from somewhere, go to Gran's cottage, make a cup of tea and feed Blackie? Then we could go straight on from there. I think I can guarantee that you'll enjoy it.'

She did. There was quite a crowd of people of all ages, some dressed in

Western outfits, others like themselves, in casual clothes. Brett steered her into the middle of the lines of dancers, so that she had someone to follow whichever way they were facing and she took it from there. She picked up the moves as they went along, and by the end of the evening, her mind was a maze of all the various instructions. At times she felt as though she had two left feet, but no-one seemed to mind, even when she ended up facing the wrong way or completely out of step with everyone else!

'I'd better get a T-shirt printed with, 'Don't follow me, I'm out of step',' Sophie quipped, with a laugh, as they sat down for a breather.

'You'll soon pick it up,' Brett replied, his eyes holding an evident softness as he looked at her.

Did that mean he wanted to see her again? She hoped so. She sat out and watched some of the more complicated dances, insisting that Brett took part. She had to admit that it all looked very impressive when the dancers swayed and moved in synchronised motion, the lines and columns flowing as one. Her heart missed more than a few beats as she watched him, thumbs hooked in his waistband, his long legs like rubber, performing the complicated movements with apparent ease and nonchalance. Was it really possible to fall in love at first sight, she wondered. She'd never thought so until now!

Her thoughts brought a faint blush to her cheeks and she realised that Brett was watching her. His eyes seemed to tell her that he, too, liked what he saw! She smiled happily. Life was good!

It was quite late when Brett dropped her off at her flat. Since he had to drive back to the other side of Bolton, where he lived in his own apartment, near to the family computer store where he worked as manager, on the outskirts of Manchester, she didn't invite him in.

'Scout nights are Mondays and Fridays,' Brett explained, as they sat in his car for a few minutes. 'I'll be able to nip in to see Gran for a few minutes but not at the regular visiting hour on those nights. Mum and Dad might be able to come down for a few flying visits, and with you helping with feeding Blackie, and a few visits to Gran when you can make it, I reckon we'll manage, don't you?'

'Yes, and thank you for tonight. I've enjoyed myself immensely.'

'Good! So have I!' he said and they smiled at each other, without either being aware that they were doing so.

It was Sophie who looked away first.

'Well, good-night, then. Thank you again for a lovely day. It's been fun.'

She was already slipping out of her seat. As she turned to shut the door, she realised that Brett had also left the car. He joined her on the pavement. He placed his hands upon her shoulders and smiled down at her upturned face.

'Do all nurses have pretty, little, turned-up noses, like you?'

'My nose doesn't turn up!'

'Yes, it does! I like it. It's cute! It does

strange and wonderful things to me, like making me want to kiss you.'

He lowered his face towards hers. She could feel the warmth of his breath on her face, making her feel giddy with anticipation.

'I've been dying to do this all evening.'

She felt a stirring sensation begin deep inside her and spiral its way upwards. His lips were gentle as they moved softly over hers, increasing in pressure as he felt her response. His kiss tasted sweet and the faint fragrance of his after-shave was intoxicating. It wasn't a long kiss but they both looked pretty pleased with it.

'I'd like to see you again,' Brett said softly. 'Shall I give you a call on Tuesday to see how you are fixed?'

'Yes, that would be lovely.'

'Until Tuesday then, my red rose girl!'

He waited until she had reached the top step and unlocked the door, then, with a wave of his hand, he drove away.

With a happy smile on her just-kissed lips, Sophie ran lightly up the stairs to her rooms on the top floor. Her heart was singing. She hadn't felt this good for ages. Romance certainly put a sparkle into life, she reflected happily. As she reached the last landing, the faint sound of a baby's cry reached her ears. A hand on the banister, she paused. She didn't know there was a baby in the building. Had someone got an overnight visitor? She shrugged. It was nothing to do with her. She continued up a few more steps, until her eyes were level with the top of the stairs.

There, a cardboard box lay on the mat outside her door. As she slowly went up the few remaining steps, she could see that it contained a white-wrapped bundle — a bundle that moved and issued an ever-strengthening cry!

4

Sophie ran up the remaining steps. What was a baby doing on her doorstep? She didn't know anyone who was expecting a baby, except those on her visiting list, and she could tell at a glance it was only hours old.

She dropped down at the side of the box and carefully lifted out the precious bundle. The tiny baby's eyes seemed to fix steadfastly upon her own.

'Now, who are you?' she asked softly.

She raised the baby to her face and nestled her cheek against its face. Its lips nuzzled against her skin.

'You're hungry, aren't you? And I've nothing to give you,' she whispered gently.

Her mind was spinning ahead of itself as she replaced the tiny bundle into the box and got out her keys. She needed to phone one of the local midwives for advice, notify the police, in order to activate a search for the mother, who would almost certainly be in need of medical attention.

She would also need to think about getting some milk for the baby to drink. She'd also better make a quick check to make sure that the baby was physically all right. Something might have made its mother panic.

She washed her hands and carefully unwrapped the baby's covering. It was a white towel, with an appliquéd pink satin rose in one corner. Without consciously thinking, her mind decided that it was quite good quality towelling, which might help in tracing the mother.

The baby was a girl, and, to all initial appearances, she was perfectly formed, if a bit on the small side. Sophie guessed she must be about five and a half pounds, thinking back to her midwifery course.

She wrapped the baby up again and laid her on her sofa, then put the kettle on to boil. Cooled, boiled water would be better than nothing, so the sooner it was boiled and cooling, the better, and she'd need a small syringe to give the water to the baby. There'd be one in her bag.

She flipped open the phone book and dialled the number of the local midwife, Denise, glancing at the clock on the wall as she did so. Nearly midnight! She wasn't going to be over-popular, was she?

'Oh, Denise!' she said when the phone was answered. 'Yes, sorry to bother you at this late hour, but you'll never guess what I've just found on my doorstep! No, not a bunch of roses, and not next door's milk bottles. It's a baby! A newborn baby girl. No, of course I don't know whose it is. What I do need to know is what to do about it! Yes, if you would, and will you stop by at the all-night chemist and get some baby milk, bottles and teats? Oh, and some first-size nappies.'

What a way to end her evening! By the time Denise Robinson arrived

Sophie had warmed up her flat, given the baby a few drops of the cool, boiled water and had made herself a bracing cup of coffee.

Between them, she and Denise checked the baby over more thoroughly, bathed the tiny mite and dressed her in some second-hand baby clothes that Denise had thought to bring along. While Denise tried to get the baby to drink some milk, Sophie shook out the folded piece of sheet in the bottom of the box and found a brief note.

'Read it out,' Denise suggested.

Dear Sister Draycott, I don't know what to do with her but I know you will look after her because you are kind.

'Is that it?' Denise asked.

'Yes,' Sophie answered.

'Well, it must definitely be someone who knows you. Can't you think of anyone who was expecting a baby?'

Sophie shook her head.

'It must be someone who hasn't

registered as pregnant. We need to get some publicity on it, find out if anyone's noticed anything, possibly a teenager acting out of character. The thing is, what do we do for tonight?'

It was now one o'clock in the morning.

'How do you feel about keeping her here until morning?' Denise asked. 'Otherwise, it's a drive out to Farnworth which means you, because I'm on call.'

On Sophie's agreement, she continued.

'Right! I'll make out a report and we'll get together first thing in the morning. Have a good night!'

'Thanks! By the way, I think we'll call her Rose.'

Rose slept most of the night, which was a great relief to Sophie.

She called in at the health centre in the morning to show the precious bundle to the staff on duty and then made her way to the Princess Anne Maternity Unit at Farnworth, leaving

Denise to see to the other side of the matter.

A TV news crew had already been alerted and were there to interview her, much to her embarrassment. Still, if the publicity managed to reunite Rose with her mother, then it would be worth it.

Sophie told the interviewer how she had found the baby, and made an impassioned plea to the mother to come forward, promising confidentiality and every available help in sorting out any problems. A lunch-time appeal was to go out on all television channels, with the promise of more later in the day.

Meanwhile, the various medical practitioners sifted through their files and the local high schools were notified to keep an eye open for unexplained absences or other likely events.

Sophie remembered Blackie at lunchtime and scurried off to feed him. He twisted himself around her legs, obviously missing his owner and wanting some company. She picked him up and stroked his glossy fur for a few minutes but eventually had to put him down again. She was only halfway through her round and wanted to see what the TV interview came out like.

She looked at her list. Who wouldn't mind her being a bit cheeky and asking to see it on their television?

Mrs Millfield was down for a visit at half-past one. If she brought that visit forward, she could be with her at the right time. She gave Blackie a final cuddle.

'See you tomorrow,' she promised him. 'You'll have to make do with Brett tonight.'

Mrs Millfield was only too pleased to oblige when Sophie arrived and made her request.

'Come right in, Sister. An abandoned baby, you say? What's the world coming to? And left on your doorstep? Well, I don't know!'

Sophie felt strange watching herself on TV but Mrs Millfield was suitably impressed.

'And what a lovely baby! Just look at her!'

'We called her Rose,' Sophie added, 'but the main thing is, we need to find the mother.'

Sophie was back on her rounds before she remembered she had forgotten to ask Mrs Millfield about her daughter, Emma. The girl hadn't come to see her on Saturday morning. So it would be next Saturday before she was able to come again, unless she scheduled her visit to see Mrs Millfield after school hours one day.

That was a worthy consideration. She jotted it down in her diary. Now, who was next?

At the end of the day, she was glad to get home and soak in the bath. She knew Brett was calling in to see Mrs Carter that evening, albeit briefly, and didn't feel guilty about merely making a phone call to the orthopaedic ward to make sure that everything was all right. It was. So she settled herself down to do her reports and have an early night.

* * *

Next day, the baby was still unclaimed and none of the few phone calls to the help-line set up led to anything new. Even so, Sophie drove home with a light heart. Brett had promised to ring and she was looking forward to seeing him again.

She had a quick shower, sprayed a little of her favourite perfume over her, put on a calf-length blue skirt and close-fitting top and settled down to read a magazine. Brett hadn't given a time, but she was assuming they would have a bite to eat somewhere, so she didn't make herself a snack.

Time ticked on and it was after eight o'clock before she began to doubt if he was going to ring her. She waited a while longer, wondering if anything had gone wrong with Mrs Carter and he had been summoned to the hospital, but a call to the ward assured her that everything was all right in that direction.

She paced up and down her room and glanced through her window a number of times, into the street below, hoping that, for some reason, he had decided to come straight there. But her efforts were in vain. Her spirit sank. In spite of the lovely time she felt they had had together, Brett must have decided that he didn't want to see her again.

She then spent a miserable evening, listlessly flicking from channel to channel on her television and eventually turning it off. She tried to read a book, but couldn't remember what she had read and eventually flung it down in disgust.

Why should she let a man make her feel like this! But, she had liked him. She really had. And, she had thought he really liked her. How mistaken could you be!

★　★　★

She awoke in a better frame of mind the following day. There were lots of things that could have prevented him from ringing her, she comforted herself. Heaven forbid it was an accident! Surely not! Perhaps something to do with his work, or his parents? No, he would have phoned.

She didn't have his phone number. There hadn't been the need, so she couldn't ring him, which left Mrs Carter.

It was Wednesday, line dancing evening, so if she timed her visit properly, she wouldn't run the risk of inadvertently bumping into him at the hospital which might prove awkward. For a brief moment her mind travelled back to Sunday evening, seeing Brett, thumbs hooked in his waistband, performing a series of fascinating moves, his body perfectly controlled as he turned and twisted. Her heart flipped and sank at the same time. It hurt. Why? What had she done wrong?

She shook away the thoughts as she fixed her hair. This time last week she hadn't known him, so he couldn't have left her life in tatters, could he? There were plenty of other equally-attractive men out there, except the thought of them didn't do much to soothe her aching heart. Right now, she only wanted Brett, but, for some reason, he didn't want her.

Her professionalism put her private life on hold once she stepped outside her door and, if anyone noticed her slightly preoccupied mind, they put it down to concern over baby Rose. The mother hadn't yet come forward and everyone involved knew that, some-where, someone, probably a young girl, was going through a time of personal torment.

The day seemed endless but, at last, Sophie went home for a quick meal. Not knowing the exact time of the line dancing, she decided that if she went to see Rose first, she could drop in to see Mrs Carter at about eight o'clock. That should give her a clear field, and she could take it from there.

Rose was a picture of health and

beauty. How could anyone not want to claim her? Yet, Sophie knew that there were many reasons why the mother might have felt unable to rear the child — and the decision to abandon her would not have come lightly.

But, much as she felt compassion and concern for the mother, the mere sight of Rose laid claim to her own aching heart. For a fleeting second, she wished she could pick her up and take her home and wrap her life around her, but she knew that could never be.

It was only a short hop from the baby unit to the main building. Sophie's stomach felt cramped with nerves. What would she do or say if Brett were there?

She anxiously scanned the length of the ward. To her great relief, there were no visitors by Mrs Carter's bed. She willed a bright smile on her face and walked briskly down the ward.

'Sister Draycott! I didn't expect to see you again so soon,' Mrs Carter exclaimed. 'You must have a lot of better things to do than visit an old woman like me. Not that I'm not pleased to see you! Of course, I am. It were grand to see you on TV Monday night wi' that baby. A real beauty she is and no mistake!'

Sophie sat down by her bed and, after enquiring about Mrs Carter's own health and progress, re-told the whole story, omitting whom she had been with just prior to the event. She didn't want to spoil their rapport this early in her visit.

She knew she would have to say something eventually, but it was difficult to know just what. She waited until she had risen to go.

'Er . . . is Brett all right?' she asked, as casually as she could, feeling her cheeks warm.

'Aye. He were in earlier on. Brought me this lovely bowl of fruit, he did,' Mrs Carter replied.

Sophie's eyes followed her glance to the bedside locker, where a bowl of fresh fruit sat in front of a vase of red roses. What had Brett called her? His red rose girl? Huh! That hadn't lasted long, had it?

'He brought the roses last night,' Mrs Carter continued. 'He's a good lad. Make someone a fine husband, he will.'

Her eyes seemed to look at Sophie. Sophie nodded glumly. She decided to take a chance of humiliation.

'Yes. I liked him. We had a nice evening out on Sunday.'

'Aye, I thought you and he might . . . '

Mrs Carter stopped and pressed her lips together.

'Still, it's not to be, so I mustn't interfere. He wondered about Blackie, whether or not you would still see to him.'

Glad of something to seize on to, Sophie quickly agreed.

'Oh, yes, that's all right. Tell him I'll feed him every morning, as arranged.'

She leaned over to kiss the old lady's cheek.

'Now I really must go. I'll call in again when I'm passing. So you just get on with getting better and we'll soon have you home again. 'Bye.'

Hoping that she had concealed how upset she felt, Sophie hurried away. So Brett had decided not to contact her again. It was a cruel blow. She had hoped for a plausible reason for his failure to ring her, something to restore her self-worth, but, it wasn't to be.

She had better forget him.

5

Over the next few days, Sophie threw herself into her job. There were other people out there with real problems and genuine needs, not just pathetic creatures like herself who fell apart after an extremely brief romantic interlude.

In spite of calling to see Mrs Millfield at four o'clock several times and even later on some days, she didn't coincide with Emma coming home from school.

'Is Emma avoiding me?' she asked one day.

'You know what teenagers are like,' Mrs Millfield replied. 'Besides, she's looking a lot better. I think she must be seeing to a diet herself. I just hope she isn't overdoing it. She's gone awful moody recently. Oh, and I nearly forgot, she bought this to give to that baby you found. She said she and her friends had clubbed together for it. Isn't that thoughtful of them?'

She handed Sophie a large pink and white rabbit.

'She said it could sit in the baby's cot and make her feel she belongs to someone.'

'Oh, that's nice. Tell her thank you, won't you?'

A number of gifts had arrived, following the television item. Most of them had been scattered around the maternity unit. Rose was doing well. The authorities would have to be thinking about foster parents for her soon. Sophie knew she would miss her. She popped in to see her whenever she could, occasionally going on to see Mrs Carter, always making sure that her visits were at a time when Brett wouldn't be there. She wasn't sure she could cope with seeing him yet.

She caught sight of Robert one day. He was coming out of the council offices, looking rather pleased with himself. She felt sure he had recognised her car but didn't make any move to acknowledge her. That was fine by her. She had no regrets in that direction. But it did set her off thinking about a new car.

She thought of the wonderful feeling of the wind blowing back her hair in Brett's convertible, and made an instant decision. She would buy a new car, a soft-top, sporty model. There! She felt better already!

Mrs Carter continued to recover well physically. Her ulcers were healing and her ankle mending. Uncertain of how capable she would be regards to mobility and looking after herself once discharged from hospital, Sophie hesitated to mention any doubts about her being able to return home. It would be time enough when the time drew nearer.

In the meantime, the main thing was to keep her spirits up. It was obvious to all that Mrs Carter was fretting about Blackie.

'I really do miss him, you know, and I'm sure he's missing me.'

'I'm sure he is, but he's fine, honestly. I see him every day.'

Sophie had an idea. It would have to be her day off, which was Thursday this week, which was all to the good, she reflected, as Brett would be calling at the usual visiting hour, by which time she would be gone. She borrowed a cat basket and put the reluctant Blackie inside it. She put the basket on the floor of her brand new, bright red sports car and drove over to the hospital.

Mrs Carter was sitting in the rest-room.

'Come on. I've got a surprise for you,' Sophie said with a smile.

With the help of a nurse, they got Mrs Carter into a wheelchair and pushed her along to an empty side ward. She made sure the door and window were shut, unsure how Blackie would react to sudden release from his short captivity, then lifted the basket on to Mrs Carter's lap. Mrs Carter's face was already shining in anticipation.

'Carefully, now,' Sophie warned as

she unfastened the clasp and slightly raised the lid. 'Talk to him. Get him used to the sound of your voice.'

'Eeh, Blackie! Blackie, love! It's me. Come to mother!'

Her voice wobbled and tears appeared in her eyes, but her face was alight. She slipped a hand through the narrow gap and felt his fur, stroking him and talking to him.

'I think he'll be all right now, love,' she said to Sophie.

She grasped him firmly and lifted him out. Sophie wept tears of joy with her, as she cuddled her precious pet. Blackie lay full length up Mrs Carter's body, kneading her ample chest with his front paws, purring loudly.

'Oh, I can't thank you enough, Sophie, love. You've made my day and that's for sure.'

'I only wish I'd thought of it sooner, but now I have, I'll bring him again,' Sophie assured her.

She was reluctant to break into the contented scene but knew that she had to. Brett would be arriving at his gran's cottage soon, expecting to find a hungry cat, so she needed to get him back there.

Mrs Carter reluctantly handed him over.

'All good things come to an end,' she remarked philosophically, nuzzling her face one last time into his soft fur. 'But I feel heaps better for having seen him. You're a kind girl.'

She reached out and squeezed Sophie's hand. Neither of them heard the door open.

'So here you are!'

It was only when he spoke that Sophie whirled round.

'Brett!'

She clutched Blackie to her chest, thankful to have him in her arms as a sort of barrier between them. She felt her face go hot and cold. And she knew that her heart was beating so erratically that she was afraid it would burst. Brett nodded in her direction.

'Sophie.'

He, too, looked taken aback, as if he didn't quite know what to do or say next. Sophie wasn't sure how long they simply stared at each other. It felt like hours but must have only been a few seconds.

Sophie tried to take control of herself. Seeing him there was just too much for her. His eyes held a hesitant look, and yet shone with a light that she couldn't quite determine. Almost hopeful? Pleasurable? No, it couldn't be. He was surprised, that was all, just as she was. And his pleasure was simply relief at finding Blackie was safe.

She was afraid that her voice would betray her emotions. She thrust Blackie at him.

'You may as well take Blackie home, then he can stay a bit longer. Leave the basket at the cottage. I'll bring him again.'

She knew she was gabbling.

'Goodbye, Mrs Carter. I'll call again.'

She didn't dare look at Brett. She knew she hadn't felt able to face him so soon, but, even so, she hadn't expected his presence to affect her as badly as this. Her reaction completely unnerved her.

It was only when she was seated in her car that she recalled his parting words to her as she fled.

'Goodbye. I hope you'll be very happy.'

What exactly did he mean by that?

When Sophie looked at her list the following day, she made up her mind that, come what may, she was going to see Emma Millfield that afternoon. She wasn't sure what niggled at her, but there was something that wouldn't let go, in spite of the fact that her mother said she was starting to lose some weight.

The girl had been avoiding her, whereas she had formerly been a friendly girl, especially since she had been on Sophie's list. There had to be a reason for her sudden aversion.

She wasn't due to make a visit that day. Mrs Millfield's burns were healing nicely, but it gave her the excuse she needed. It was Emma who came to the door.

The way the girl's face changed colour, as she realised who their visitor was, confirmed Sophie's suspicions that she had been avoiding her. However, she didn't want to confront her on the doorstep.

'Hello, Emma. Is your mother in? I was passing by and thought I would just pop in to see her.

'Oh . . . er . . . hello. Yes, she's in the kitchen.'

'Good. Here, hold my bag for me, whilst I take my coat off, will you, there's a good girl?'

Anything to keep the girl from running off, which is what she looked like doing. As she spoke, Mrs Millfield emerged from the kitchen, drying her hands on a towel.

'Sorry to be a nuisance, Mrs Millfield,' Sophie continued, trying to silently convey with her eyes that she really wanted to speak to Emma. 'I know it's getting on for tea-time, but I was passing by and it will help my list tomorrow.'

Mrs Millfield nodded, with a look of understanding.

'That's all right, Sister. I know how busy you get.'

Sophie noticed that Emma had indeed lost weight since she had last seen her. In fact, she had lost that much that her face was showing the strain.

She was not the happy child Sophie had known a few months ago. Sophie wanted to keep her in the room.

'Thank you for the cuddly rabbit you bought for Rose, Emma. It was very kind of you. I've put it in her cot, like you said.'

Emma made a strange sound, like a strangled sob. With her hand clasped across her mouth, she leaped to her feet and ran from the room. Sophie stared after her.

'What . . . '

Mrs Millfield made for the door.

'Come back, Emma. Don't you run

off like that! I'm sorry, Sister. I'll fetch her back to apologise to you.'

Sophie reached out and halted her.

'No. Leave her be.'

At the same moment, she noticed the towel that Mrs Millfield had dropped on the end of the sofa. It was a white one, with a pink satin rose appliquéd in one corner. Sophie stared at it, knowing what the answer was before she had had time to properly formulate the thought.

Of course! That was it! Emma's weight gain — and sudden loss of it! Why hadn't she suspected something long before now?

'May I go upstairs to Emma?' she asked.

'Yes, of course, love. I don't know what's got into her these days. She didn't used to be like this.'

Sophie went upstairs, following the sounds of Emma's sobs. The girl had flung herself on top of her bed, sobbing her heart out. Sophie sat beside her and laid her hand on her shoulder.

'It's all right, Emma. Cry it out.'

Eventually her sobs ceased. She twisted her head round.

'You know, don't you?'

Sophie nodded.

'I think so. Rose is your baby, isn't she?'

Emma nodded, brushing back some wet strands of hair out of her troubled eyes.

'Yes, I didn't know what to do. But I knew you would look after her for me. Does Mum know?'

'Not yet. I thought I'd better wait until I knew for sure, but we will have to tell her.'

'I know. She'll go mad, and Dad! He'll kill me!'

Emma looked petrified. Sophie put her arm around her.

'They'll be upset, and probably a bit shocked at first, but I don't think either of them will kill you! Once they're over the shock, they might even be a little bit pleased. Rose is a beautiful baby, you know.'

'Can I see her?'

'Yes, of course. And we need to make sure you are all right as well,' Sophie pointed out.

She hugged Emma to her.

'You've been through a few tough weeks. It must have been very hard for you. But, you're not on your own any more.'

'What'll happen?'

'That depends on what you and your parents decide. Er . . . do you know who the father is?'

Emma reddened and hung her head. 'Yes.'

'I, or someone else, have to ask these things. Do you think he'll be willing to help you?'

Emma shook her head.

'No. We've split up, and I don't want to involve him. He wanted me to get rid of it, but I couldn't!'

Her eyes were filled with torment, tearing at Sophie's heart.

'Do you think you might want to keep the baby?'

'I think so. I didn't think I'd want to,

but once I'd held her, I knew that I loved her. It was awful, having to give her up, but I didn't know how I'd manage. I still don't! I'll have to leave school and I'd hoped to go to university. Mum and Dad are going to be so disappointed in me.'

Her face crumbled again.

Sophie hugged her.

'Initially they might be angry and dismayed, but give them time. Remember, you've had time to think about it, they haven't! But I'll be very surprised if they don't stand by you. So, shall we get the worst part over and tell your mother?'

Emma nodded reluctantly. Sophie hesitated.

'Do you want me to tell her?'

'Will you?'

'Yes. Why don't you go along to the bathroom and rinse your face while I go downstairs and tell your mum what it's all about? I expect she'll come right up to see you.'

There were a difficult few minutes.

Mrs Millfield was astounded, disbelieving, dismayed, angry and, finally, tearful. Just as she had comforted Emma a short while ago, Sophie now comforted her mother. At last, Mrs Millfield dried her eyes.

'Where is she? I'd best see her.'

Sophie gave them ten minutes, then went upstairs to join them. There were decisions to be made and things to be done. Sophie set the ball rolling by phoning the hospital. They booked Emma to come in straight away. Sophie arranged to meet them there.

It was all very emotional. Mr Millfield had tears in his eyes when he first held his grandchild, but his face shone with pride. Sophie could imagine it wouldn't all be plain sailing.

A lot of decisions still had to be made, and a lot of adjustments would have to follow, but she left them with their arms around each other and the baby in her grandfather's arms, which was a good start. It was now up to the authorities to help them sort things out.

Back at her car, Sophie looked at her watch. It was only eight o'clock. She hadn't been to see Mrs Carter for a few days. The last she had heard was that she would soon be well enough to be discharged and was going to be assessed by the social services to determine what options were open to her. Had anything been decided yet?

Brett would be at the community hall line dancing. She shook herself crossly. Why did she still think of him? She should put him out of her mind, once and for all! And she would! Nevertheless, she would visit his grandmother. It wasn't her fault that she had a hard-hearted, fickle, drop-dead-gorgeous grandson, was it?

She knew that something was wrong the minute she entered the ward. Mrs Carter was in tears. As soon as she saw Sophie, she held out her arms to her.

'Oh, Sister Draycott, something dreadful has happened. It's Brett!'

Sophie's heart jumped. What was it?

What had happened? She rushed forward.

'He's been in an accident. He's been brought here to the hospital.'

Sophie's face froze in shock as she dropped to her knees at the side of her chair.

'What happened? Is he going to be all right?'

Mrs Carter shook her head. For a moment Sophie thought she meant that he was dead. Her heart went cold. It was with some relief that she realised that Mrs Carter was continuing.

'They say he's unconscious. They've sent for Kathleen and John, my daughter and her husband. Go and visit him, Sister, then come back and tell me how he is. They won't tell me anything, but that's worse than not knowing, isn't it?'

Sophie left in a daze.

She wasn't sure that Brett would want her to visit, but she would go, for Mrs Carter's sake.

6

Sophie wouldn't have recognised Brett. His head was bandaged and what she could see of his face was swollen and changing colour through all shades of purple. His eyes, as it happened, were closed in unconsciousness, but she didn't think they would look any different if they were open. Narrow slits would be all they were, but, from the look of him, he wouldn't be trying to open them for a while.

In stark contrast to his tanned skin, white dressings swathed his upper body. They didn't hide the firm, muscular structure and it somehow seemed incongruous to see all the tubes and attachments that were keeping him alive and monitoring his progress. Sophie knew instantly that her attempts to put Brett Ridgeway out of her mind and her life had failed. She longed to reach out to him and touch him, to impart some of her strength and vitality to him. But, even as she thought of it, she heard a nurse's voice in the corridor.

'In here, Mr and Mrs Ridgeway. Oh, hello, Sister Draycott. Er . . . are you here officially?'

Sophie forced a smile.

'Hello, Angie. Nice to see you again.'

Strange how her voice could react on a social level, whilst her mind was still stunned in immobility.

'Er . . . no, not really. Brett's grandmother is one of my district patients.'

Her eyes had travelled beyond the nurse to the anxious couple behind her, realising that they were Brett's parents. The two women exchanged glances, both instantly liking what they saw, but not realising that it was because they shared the same emotions of love and fear — the fear that Brett might not recover. They shook hands.

'Sister Draycott, my mother has

mentioned you many times. Thank you for all that you do for her, and looking after Blackie, too. It's very kind of you.'

Mrs Ridgeway spoke the words but her eyes were already fixed upon the inert figure of her son. Sophie moved aside. They would talk later, she was sure, but, right now, Brett's mother wanted to be near her son, to be the one to touch him, to hold his hand and tell his unconscious form that everything would be all right, and, although it hurt, Sophie knew that that right belonged to Mrs Ridgeway not to her. She stood apart from the little group, the others now hardly aware of her presence.

'What happened?'

It was Mr Ridgeway who spoke, asking the question that the two women had formed in their minds but had been unable to concentrate enough to voice it. The nurse shrugged, a wry grimace twisting her mouth, conveying the utter senselessness of it.

'Some boys . . . hooligans . . . louts . . . threw a concrete coping stone off a motorway bridge on to his car. It smashed straight through his windscreen, catching him full in the face and his chest. It's madness! Just what makes them do things like this?'

'I don't know,' Mrs Ridgeway said as she gently stroked her son's cheek.

Tears glistened in her eyes but she battled against them.

'It's Mum, Brett. I don't know if you can hear me, but your dad and I are here. We're staying at your gran's, so hurry up and get better. We love you.'

As her voice broke on the last words, Mr Ridgeway stepped forward and put his arm around her.

'We're right here, son, for as long as it takes.'

Over the next few days, Brett's parents sat by his bedside, together or separately, talking to the silent figure of their son, silently watching him, eager for any sign of return to consciousness. Sophie called briefly after work each day, telling herself it was for Mrs Carter that she went, but she knew it was for herself.

'Yes, I'm a friend,' she explained to his mother, wondering what Brett would say if he were conscious. 'I went to line dancing with him,' she added, not wanting Mrs Ridgeway to think that there was more between them than there was.

Mrs Carter anxiously awaited her daily visit. Sophie didn't try to hide the serious nature of Brett's condition. The old lady might be eighty-five but she was far from senile.

'He's in good hands,' Sophie assured her.

'I know, love, and thank you for keeping me up to date. I rest easier, knowing how he is. Kathleen and John try to protect me. I know they mean well, but I'd rather know. You understand, don't you?'

Sophie nodded then replied softly, 'Yes, I do.'

Mrs Carter smiled.

'I know.'

One day, Sophie had just stepped inside the side ward when the alarm bell was triggered from Brett's monitoring machine. Brett's mother leaped up from the chair at the side of his bed.

'Brett! No!'

Sophie moved swiftly, pressing the emergency button as she stepped forward. The emergency team responded quickly and arrived in the doorway as Sophie put her arms around Mrs Ridgeway's shoulders and led her aside, to give the team clear access. They were well-practised. Although it seemed like an eternity, it was less than a minute before the monitoring machine resumed its steady beep. Sophie and Mrs Ridgeway smiled at each other in delight.

There were a number of further scares, but Brett's firm, healthy body began to respond to the intensive care and enforced rest. The physiotherapist worked on his arms and legs, keeping the muscles fit. It was still pitiful to see every aspect of his being controlled by machinery and endless tubes feeding and cleansing his body.

It seemed as though the routine would go on for ever. It came as a bit of a shock, therefore, when Sophie looked up from the book she was reading out loud, to see Brett's eyes wide open and fixed unblinkingly on her face. For a second or two, she stared back, unable to think or move.

It was her day off. John Ridgeway had returned to their home in Yorkshire for a few days to see to his business, and Sophie had volunteered to give Kathleen a few hours to go to the hairdresser and do a bit of shopping, knowing from experience that carers needed some time for themselves. She desperately hoped Kathleen wouldn't mind her being the one to witness Brett's return to consciousness.

'Brett! You're awake! Oh, at last!'

Her book fell unheeded to the floor. A delighted beam lit her face. For a moment, she forgot that he hadn't wanted to continue their friendship.

She had seen so much of him over the last two weeks or so that she felt like an old friend.

'How are you feeling, Brett?'

There was no answering smile on his face. His expression remained inscrutably cool, almost impersonal, as if she meant nothing to him at all. Her heart sank and the light began to fade from her eyes, as she took in the severity of his expression. He was not pleased to see her. It had been a great mistake to keep coming, hoping.

His lips were moving but she couldn't make out the sounds. She put her ear nearer to his mouth.

'Oh, you're thirsty? Of course.'

She quickly poured some water into a spout-beaker and held it to his lips.

'Is that better?'

She felt nervous, made unsure of herself by his lack of reaction.

'Who are you?' he whispered.

She had moved across to press the bell to summon a nurse, but she was halted by his words. She stared at him uncertainly, as he slowly formed his lips to repeat the words.

'Do I know you?'

'Yes, that is . . . I'm called Sophie.'

'Sophie?'

He repeated her name softly, staring fixedly at her face, a puzzled frown creasing his forehead. His gaze left her face and slowly travelled around the room. He passed his tongue over his dry lips.

'Where are we? Is this a hospital?'

'Yes. You had an accident. You've been quite poorly.'

He accepted her words without question. For a minute he was silent. Sophie watched his face anxiously. He seemed to be at a loss what to say.

'I'll get the nurse, Brett, and your mother will be back soon.'

'Is that my name? Brett?'

'Yes.'

He looked puzzled.

'I seem to have forgotten everything,' he said and panic was creeping into his voice and across his face.

'It's all right. Don't worry. It's often the way, after a head injury. It will all come back to you. I'll fetch a nurse.'

The doctor told John and Kathleen exactly the same later on that day.

'Head injuries are always unpredictable. There has been severe trauma to Brett's body, especially to his head. Our bodies are wonderfully made, but don't always react as we expect them to. But, don't worry. More often than not, everything comes right eventually.'

They were to hang on to those words over the next few days. When they ran response tests on Brett it was discovered that he had completely lost the use of his legs.

7

Sophie's life had become a hectic whirl of activity. During the daytime, her job came first and she devoted as much time, care and energy to it as she ever had done. But, once she was off duty, she showered and changed and drove straight to the hospital.

John Ridgeway came and went as his business affairs allowed him. Kathleen stayed on in her mother's cottage, though she knew that was on a limited time basis, as she worked in the family business on the administration side. She would soon be having to make a decision over whether to get back to work or to decide to resign to look after Brett.

Mrs Carter was another pressing matter. Her ankle was mending nicely and the leg ulcers had cleared up. A social worker had given her assessment that she needed to be in care somewhere, but, as yet, this had met only resistance from the old lady.

'What do you want to do?' Sophie asked, in her official capacity as district nurse. 'You could go into a residential home.'

'But what about Blackie? I've missed him for long enough. I know our Kathleen's looking after him all right, but we need to be back together. No-one else needs me, but he does!'

'Well, what about sheltered accommodation? There, you would have your independence but still have someone on hand to be around in case of emergencies, and you could keep Blackie!'

Mrs Carter considered it. Sophie knew she was weakening.

'But I still don't really want to leave my cottage. It's been my home for so long, ever since Jack and I were wed. It's seen some happenings, it has.'

'I know. I do understand, but, it's not really a good option for you. It's cold in winter, no central heating and it has steep stairs and cold bedrooms. The only toilet is upstairs and that's not convenient. What if you fall again?'

Mrs Carter looked at her shrewdly.

'Would you like to live there?'

Sophie was rather taken aback. She had never considered it. She looked at Mrs Carter's expectant face. The old lady loved her home. She would probably expect everyone else to love it, too, and there was no doubt that it was a very pleasant cottage. Sophie smiled.

'Yes, it's a lovely place. It could be made more modern, without destroying its charm or character. I suppose it needs someone with a genuine love for it and a vision to only change what is necessary.'

'Someone like you, you mean?'

'Oh, I wouldn't just say like me, but, yes, someone young and just starting out. It would make a nice family home.'

Mrs Carter nodded.

'Yes, you're right.'

She looked sad for a moment, as she

weighed her decision then brightened visibly.

'You're right! Yes, I'll sell it, and move into one of those shelters. I just hope they're better than the ones they tried to get us to move into during the last war. Dreadful places, they were!'

Sophie smiled.

'Kathleen and John will find you a nice place. Maybe one near them, if you like, or one not too far from here, if you would rather be near your friends. Wherever, it will be one where Blackie will be welcome.'

Kathleen was pleased when she learned of her mother's decision.

'We've been trying to get her to move for years,' she confided, 'but never got anywhere with her. We'll see to it at once, before she changes her mind. In fact, a young man called at the cottage about a week ago, asking if the cottage was going to be up for sale. He left his card. I'll get a valuation then ring to ask him if he is still interested. You never know, it might be quite straightforward.'

They had arranged to give Brett his late-afternoon therapy session themselves. The two women got on well together and Kathleen was glad of Sophie's assistance.

'He responds more to you, and doesn't complain half so much,' she said with a wry laugh. 'I'm just his old mum.'

It was true. Brett was rather surly at times. Sophie knew that it was because of the pain he was in and the frustration caused by his lack of memory and paralysis of his legs. Although everyone hoped that it would be only temporary, nobody knew for certain. And it didn't take much imagination to realise what the thought of that would do to a previously healthy young man. She had seen the tortured look in his eyes when any of his scouts came in, or any other friends. Everyone sympathised, but at the end of their visit, they got up and walked away. Brett's eyes were a misery to see.

However, Sophie merely laughed now in return.

'I'm probably more used to handling awkward patients, and they don't come much more awkward than Brett!'

'Do you mind not discussing my finer points within my hearing,' Brett objected with a rare grin. 'I don't know how I survive with two women like you constantly going on at me. You're worse than that pretty little nurse who comes to give me my massage, and she packs a punch, I can tell you.'

'Good for her!' Sophie retorted. 'Now, let's get on with these leg exercises, before we run out of time.'

She was glad that she had completed a course on physiotherapy before she had decided to settle on district nursing. Now, in conjunction with the hospital physiotherapist, she was able to supplement his exercises, keeping his muscles toned up. She showed Kathleen what to do and they gave him a strenuous half-hour work-out.

'I'm going for a cup of tea,' Kathleen

announced at the end of it. 'So don't get up to any mischief whilst I'm gone.'

'Mischief?'

Brett smiled humourlessly at Sophie, as his mother departed with a wave.

'I should be so lucky!'

His eyes glimmered briefly with mischief, his former sparkle returning, as he took hold of her hand and pulled her closer.

'I tell you what. I don't feel tempted to do this with any of the other pretty nurses.'

His eyes, sombre now, held hers for a moment or two, then he drew her closer again. Her heart began to beat rapidly. She knew he was going to kiss her. Her lips tingled in anticipation and parted slightly. She lowered her mouth to his. His lips were firm, yet gentle as he, tentatively at first, then more strongly, moved his mouth to hers. It tasted sweet and sent an ecstasy of hot fire running through her body. His hand held her head to his, his fingers twining through her loosened hair.

As they parted, Brett groaned in a mixture of pleasure and despair.

'That felt good, though I don't think my ribs think so!'

He breathed rapidly a few times, wincing as he did so. Her slightly pink cheeks and shining eyes told him that the pleasure was mutual. His voice was breathless as he continued.

'I've been longing to do that for the last few days, but I wasn't sure how you felt, whether or not you would want me to. Just look at me. I haven't much to offer anyone at the moment, have I?'

There was such bitterness in his voice. Sophie's heart went out to him. She felt weak at her knees and was glad to perch on the edge of his bed.

'That was plenty to be going on with,' she said lightly.

She could still feel the pressure of his lips upon hers and she was sure he could hear her heart beating. His kiss was everything she remembered and had longed for. He cocked his head to one side and looked at her quizzically.

'Just how friendly were we?' he asked. 'That kiss felt just right, and seems to stir memories somewhere deep within me. No other pretty young ladies have been beating on my door. Were you and I . . . '

He left the question unfinished, and Sophie felt her smile freezing on her face. What should she tell him? She could hardly say that he hadn't seemed to have been particularly fond of her before, because he would wonder why she came to see him so much. And she still didn't know why he had suddenly decided not to see her again.

'We . . . er . . . only went out together a couple of times. We met at your gran's house, when she fell down her stairs. We had a meal together, and, the following day, you took me line dancing with you.'

Honesty was the best approach.

'Line dancing? I'm not sure . . . '

'It doesn't matter. Don't worry about things you can't remember. The doctor says it will probably come back gradually. Anyway, once we get you up and walking again, I'm sure you will soon pick it up again. You were very good at it.'

'So, we were just starting a relationship, were we? That's good. I mean there isn't much I've forgotten.'

Sophie smiled weakly. There was something he'd forgotten — and she couldn't help him to remember it, but when he did, would she lose him all over again?

* * *

Brett's condition gradually stabilised. His ribs and chest wounds, and his physical head injuries were healing nicely. Emotionally though, it was a different matter. He suffered frequent bouts of despair, that his memory and leg paralysis showed no signs of resolving themselves. Some days, even Sophie's cheerful face and demeanour couldn't break through. There were times that she wondered why she bothered, except she knew that this wasn't the real Brett, the one she had fallen in love with.

'Leave me alone,' he flatly declared one day. 'I'm no use to anyone, not even you.'

He turned away from her and faced the wall.

'Take him home,' the doctor eventually suggested to John and Kathleen. 'Who knows, his home surroundings might well trigger his memory and a private nurse and physiotherapist can do as much for him as we're able to. That's what you've been badgering me about for the past week, so, go ahead. You have my full support and approval.'

'Going home?' Sophie's voice echoed, when told of the move.

'Yes, we think it best,' Kathleen affirmed.

Sophie felt the bottom sink out of her world. She had known that he would recover one day, and that with the return of his memory, their relationship might end once more. But she had hoped they would have consolidated their friendship by then, and that whatever it was that had caused him to leave her before would be irrelevant. She felt devastated.

Kathleen's face suddenly brightened.

'I wonder . . . '

She paused as if uncertain how to continue.

'I don't suppose you would consider coming to work with Brett, be his physiotherapist. We can afford to pay. I know it would mean you leaving your present job, but we would make it worth your while.'

Sophie was tempted, very much so. But Brett hadn't been very communicative towards her since the paralysis of his legs showed no signs of abating. He was taking it very badly, or was his memory returning and he had remembered the reason why he had decided to cut short their relationship?

She shook her head as she raised her eyes to meet Kathleen's eager gaze.

'I don't think it would be a very good idea. I'm sorry.'

Her voice was reluctant. Did she hope that Kathleen would try to persuade her to change her mind? She wasn't sure but she had to admit to a slight disappointment when Kathleen didn't pursue the matter.

'Maybe it's as well,' she agreed. 'It's quite all right. I understand.'

Sophie nodded numbly. Brett must have said something to his mother. She just wished she knew what it was that had caused him to turn from her.

'I hope he gets better soon. I'm sure he will.'

She was close to tears. A shadow of worry flickered across Kathleen's face.

'Yes, thank you. I hope you're right.'

She reached out to squeeze Sophie's hand.

'I know he's turned a bit surly towards you, but I can't help feeling that it's not what he really feels. He's like that with us all. You will keep in touch, won't you?'

Sophie nodded silently, not trusting herself to speak. She wasn't sure how she would cope with losing him a second time.

Sophie really missed him in the weeks that followed. She realised that she had allowed herself to dream and had come to believe in her dream. It wasn't easy to let go. She flung herself into her work. Her friends at the health centre watched her almost frenzied activity with alarm. She found solace in her work whilst the pain in her heart refused to go away.

She consulted her list and her watch one busy afternoon. Half-past four, not too bad. She would call on Mrs Carter, who had successfully moved to a flat in Willowbank Court. The two-storey building was set in beautiful grounds, quite near the town centre, making it easy for those who were still fit enough to do their own shopping to be able to do so. There was a community room, a laundrette and an on-site care worker, who contacted each resident first thing every morning and last thing every night.

'Her voice comes from there,' Mrs Carter informed Sophie, pointing up to a little speaker on the wall. 'I always put my teeth in first.'

Sophie couldn't help laughing, reaching over to tickle Blackie, who had also settled in nicely.

'Don't worry about what you look like. Mrs Collins can't really see you!'

'She can, you know! She always says, 'Well, I can see you're all right, Mrs Carter.' Any road, I'll keep on smiling, just in case!'

'You do that, Mrs Carter. It's the best way. Anyway, I'll call again next week.'

She paused in the doorway.

'Oh, I nearly forgot. Have you finalised your house sale yet?'

'Not yet, but don't worry. It's all going ahead. It'll be all signed up before the big day.'

Sophie's query as to which big day that was died on her lips. Her attention had been caught by a car which had drawn up outside the building. Its driver got out and reached into the back seat to pick up a large bunch of flowers. His male passenger got out and straightened up. It was Robert Williams! Now, whom would he be visiting here? Not that it was anything to do with her what he chose to do any more. Shrugging wryly, Sophie turned her attention back to Mrs Carter and smiling made her farewell.

She met the two men in the entrance area. Robert seemed slightly taken aback as she stepped through the swing doors, almost guilty-looking, she thought in surprise. What was he up to? She now recognised the other man. She had seen him at some political social evenings, someone Robert always seemed keen to impress. Robert swiftly regained his poise.

'Sophie! Are you keeping well?' he stammered rather awkwardly, Sophie thought.

'Yes, thank you, Robert. And you?'

Sophie included his companion in

her smile. He nodded briefly back to her. Now what was his name? Hardman? Hardcastle? It was something like that. Never mind. It wasn't important. She and Robert regarded each other silently. It was strange to have so little to say to each other, though, when she considered it, they had never really talked deeply about anything, apart from his aspirations to become more involved in politics.

'Fine,' he replied. 'I was sorry to hear of your new boyfriend's accident. Very unfortunate.'

Robert's smile didn't quite reach his eyes, Sophie noticed, wondering how she had ever thought they had anything in common.

'Yes,' she replied shortly. 'Are you here on business or pleasure?'

Robert raised one eyebrow. Sophie reddened and inwardly squirmed. It was none of her business really.

'You don't have the monopoly on doing good turns, my dear, even if we lesser mortals don't receive an accolade on television! But don't let us detain you. I'm sure your time is precious.'

His cool detachment put her at a disadvantage. He was holding the door open, obviously waiting for her to leave.

'Goodbye, Robert.'

He wasn't worth getting annoyed over. When she looked back they had gone.

The following days merged into one another and it was almost a week later before she returned to visit Mrs Carter. The old lady wasn't looking too happy.

'I've just had a letter from Kathleen,' she explained. 'It seems Brett isn't making the progress they had hoped for, and two nurses from an agency have left already. It's a pity things didn't work out between him and you. I told our Kathleen that you'd have been just the right one for him, but, still, that can't be helped, can it? You've got your own life to live.'

Sophie wished she could ask Mrs Carter if she knew what had gone wrong between them but it didn't seem right to involve a patient in a private matter. Instead, her eye was taken with the vase of flowers, standing on a corner table. Weren't they the ones she had seen Robert's companion holding last week?

'Has Robert been to see you?' she asked.

'What? Oh! Yes, he did.'

She followed Sophie's glance to the flowers.

'Er . . . a private matter. I'm sure you understand.'

She looked a bit uncomfortable, not upset, more in suppressed excitement.

'I can't say any more, swore me to secrecy, he did. You'll find out.'

At that, she pressed her lips together, tapping the side of her nose and said no more.

Sophie was intrigued. She had nothing to do with Robert any more, so what could it be? However, Mrs Carter obviously didn't want to be drawn any further and Sophie didn't believe in putting people under pressure, so the subject was dropped.

A letter from Kathleen was in her letter-box on her return home that evening.

She skimmed through the opening lines, until she reached the main subject of the letter.

Please, Sophie, will you reconsider becoming Brett's private nurse? she read. *The two we have had, so far, from an agency, have proved to be far from satisfactory, not entirely their own fault, I must admit. Brett is being far from co-operative and seems to take delight in making things difficult for everyone. I suppose he had nothing else to do.*

However, he is the one I am concerned about, so I am willing to plead with you. I'm sure you have the calibre and right personality to make headway with Brett's condition. You will not lose out financially. We will agree to any reasonable salary and contract, because I know that it will involve you either resigning from your present job or taking an unpaid break. Please, please, please, don't turn down this plea immediately. Give it your earnest consideration! We await your reply.

Sophie realised that she had been holding her breath as she read, and now she let it out with a heartfelt sigh.

What should she do?

8

Brett was sitting in his wheelchair, staring disconsolately out into the garden through the open patio windows, but he made no move, nor had he any desire to go out there. What was the point? What had flowering shrubs and climbing clematis and roses to do with him?

His eyes remained clouded. He didn't want to manoeuvre his wheelchair through the patio door on to the flower-laden patio! He couldn't care less about the newly-created decking that had been specially installed to provide a ramp down which he could safely negotiate his wheelchair. All he wanted to do was to be able to get up out of the thing and walk out of this house, get in his car and drive back to wherever it was he worked, and get on with whatever it was that he did there!

He clenched both fists in frustration and banged them both down on the arms of his chair. Why did no-one seem to understand? Why did they keep on trying to treat him like a child, regardless of the fact that he was acting like one?

Just because he couldn't remember his past or use his legs like anyone else didn't mean that he had the mind of a three-year-old, did it? Nor did it mean that he was immune to embarrassment at his lack of privacy!

Any minute now, his mother was going to be ushering in a new nurse. Why couldn't they leave him alone and let him sink in misery, since that was all that was left for him? With a determined push at his wheels, he swung the chair around, to where he could reach the cords that adjusted the vertical blinds.

He savagely hauled them across the wide patio opening, giving them the final pull that turned the individual strips flat against each other. That was better! That suited his mood.

Maybe he dozed, he wasn't sure, but, suddenly, the door opened and he was startled into wakefulness.

'Brett, dear! You're in the dark!'

His mother's voice roused him.

'I like it this way,' he said, intending to sound patient, but, even to his own ears, his voice sounded more petulant than patient.

'Guess who's come to see you?' his mother said brightly.

Why did she have to think she must always sound cheerful? He grimaced, barely looking up. No doubt it was another well-meaning friend of his mother's.

It seemed that most of his friends lived nearer to Bolton and Manchester or in some other part of the country and only a few made the required journey. That was one thing he was thankful for. He didn't want to see them, and none had yet made a return visit!

'Hello, Brett.'

The sound of her voice seemed to stop his heart beating.

'Sophie!'

His initial delight turned sour. Hadn't he made it plain to her that she was wasting her time on him?

'Why have you come?' he demanded roughly.

'Brett!'

His mother's voice sounded hurt.

'It's all right, Kathleen,' Sophie hastened to reassure her. 'It doesn't matter.'

'Why are you always so damned understanding all the time?' he said really snappily.

He'd uttered the harsh words before they had properly formed in his mind. He was ashamed to see a faint flush cover her face. For a moment, she seemed uncertain of herself. Then he saw her visibly pull herself together.

'My, you are touchy today!'

She stepped forward quickly and took hold of the hand-rests of his wheelchair.

'Draw the blinds back, will you, Kathleen? Brett can show me round the garden. It looked lovely from what I could see from the front.'

She took the wheelchair backwards over the slightly-raised step.

'I may as well start as I mean to go on!' she declared cheerfully.

Brett jerked his head round, so that he could see her face.

'Why do I get the feeling that I'm not going to like this?'

Sophie returned his gaze coolly.

'Like it or not, you're stuck with me for the next few weeks or so! I'm your new nurse, Brett, no matter what you may think.'

'You're what?'

'I'll brew us a pot of tea?' Kathleen called out to them, through the open windows. 'Half an hour!'

'Lovely!'

Sophie smiled back at her, briefly casting her eyes upwards, to convey her relief at getting the first hurdle over.

'We'll be back.'

Sophie could sense Brett's discomfort, even antagonism, as she carefully wheeled him down the decking. She had taken three days over her decision whether or not to accept John's and Kathleen's plea to become Brett's nurse. Even now, she wasn't one hundred per cent sure that she had made the right decision.

She had some unused leave and had used it to give immediate notice, deciding that, if it didn't work out, a change of job wouldn't be a bad thing. She would be able to get another job relatively easy with her qualifications, even if it meant going abroad.

A complete change would do her good. However, that was looking ahead, and for the moment, she meant to put her all into getting Brett back to his feet. Right now, that didn't look quite so simple, not if he was going to be antagonistic towards her. Still, she had known the initial meeting would be awkward.

The garden was beautiful. It was easy

to comment on the abundance of colour and variety of plants. She didn't know a lot about gardens but that didn't stop her admiring the beauty of what was there. Brett's initial monosyllabic replies gradually lengthened. She made no reference to his disability, treating him exactly as if he were strolling along by her side. When they paused, overlooking a stream, she left Brett to manoeuvre his wheelchair and leaned her arms on the top rail of the bridge, staring into the water for a few moments.

'Oh, there's a fish! Look! Did you see it?'

She turned to face him, her face alight with the unexpected pleasure. Brett smiled in return, before he had time to check himself.

'You can still smile, then?' Sophie observed, knowing that she was taking a chance, but determined not to be acting a charade.

If she had to watch what she said all the time, life would be impossible.

'There's not much to smile about!'

'Don't be so full of self-pity,' Sophie returned swiftly. 'Look at you. You can use your arms. You can move your head and neck. You can speak. You can think. Even if you never made any improvement, you would still be able to live a thoroughly meaningful life. Try being grateful for what you have instead of concentrating on what you haven't!'

Brett's hands gripped the arms of his wheelchair.

'I'm a cripple, Sophie! A useless cripple! I've got a near-useless body, and a totally useless mind. I've forgotten all I ever knew. I'm a man without a past, and, as far as I can see, a man with no future.'

'Don't give up so easily. You know what the doctors said. There's no physical reason why you can't walk.'

'So what kind of idiot does that make me? There's nothing wrong with me, but I can neither walk, nor remember anything leading up to the accident.'

He thumped his fists down on the

end of the arm rests.

'It will come. I'm sure it will. We've got to be patient.'

'Patient!'

He made a lop-sided smile.

'I can't imagine why people in my position are expected to be patient, can you? Patient by name, but not by nature.'

'What did your previous nurses do with you?'

'Exercises and massage on my legs. Looking at endless photographs of my childhood for my mind, all of which was extremely boring. The first one read me excerpts of children's classics. I told her I'd rather she read Mills and Boon to me, but she wasn't amused!'

Sophie grinned.

'I'll bear that in mind when I go to the library.'

'The library comes to us out here. Ask my mother to tell you when.'

Sophie looked at him carefully.

'How do you know that?'

'What?'

'That the library comes to the house.'

She saw his face freeze in shock.

'I don't know. I just don't know. Do you think . . . '

Sophie nodded, anticipating his words.

'I don't know for sure, but it could be that your memory is starting to come back. I think we'll concentrate on your legs and let your memory mend itself for a while. What do you say?'

'Do I have a say?'

'Only if you agree!'

'I get the feeling that I'm not going to be able to chase you away quite so fast as the others!'

9

The first thing Sophie did was to set up the adjustable massage table out of doors. It was light but strong and she could handle it easily by herself. Brett glowered at her.

'I prefer to be inside.'

'It's better for you out here.'

'Who says?'

'I do.'

'Bossy, are you?'

'When I need to be! So, come on. Move over here and let me see how well you manage to get on to the table.'

Their eyes met in silent challenge. It was Brett who gave way. With a disgruntled moan, he manoeuvred his wheelchair alongside the massage table.

Sophie had set it in a lowered position and locked its wheels. She purposely didn't attempt to help him. Instead, she busied herself setting out a tray of massage oils, waiting to see whether he could manage by himself or ask for help.

After a silent pause, Brett struggled out of his chair and heaved himself sideways on to the massage table. Sophie felt a tremor ripple inside her, as he took the weight of his body on to his arms, his muscles rippling in the sunlight. His upper body was good to look at.

'I thought you were here to help,' he grumbled peevishly as he struggled on.

'Only with things you can't do. I thought you wanted independence.'

'Independence from all this!'

He swept a baleful look at his wheelchair and the rest of the equipment she had brought outside with her.

'Give it time. It will come.'

'Huh!'

He looked suspiciously at the box of oils that she placed on a trolley at the side of the massage table.

'What's all that? Am I going to smell like some basket of roses?' he growled.

'Quite possibly, amongst other things. You'll be surprised at the effect of the different oils. I had a good chat to the physiotherapist at the hospital before I came here and I've been reading a few books on the subject. So, I have brought a selection of various essential oils that I think will be helpful to you.'

'Huh! Sounds a bit mumbo-jumbo to me! So, what am I to expect today?'

'I think a general stimulating massage will be a good way to start. See if we can get your blood surging through your veins again,' she said with a bit of a twinkle in her eyes.

'I hope you know what you might be stirring up for yourself!'

Sophie grinned.

'I've got a jug of cold water to hand, so watch your step!'

She began with vigour. The blend of oils filled her nostrils. With long, slow strokes she started on his back. She pushed and pummelled, working with an intuitive rhythm. She could feel the tension going out of them. Lower down his back, she was gentler. This was where any damaged muscles might lie.

The backs of his long legs came next. The muscles were looser, looser than they had been when she had worked on him in the hospital. She frowned at the deterioration that had occurred. This was where the real work had to be done, to tone up the muscles, ready for when he would use them again.

For a moment, she faltered. What if this were all in vain? Would he ever get up and walk again, go line dancing, go back to his scouting? Was she building up false hopes within him and his parents?

★　★　★

Every day, twice a day, she massaged and exercised his limbs, working hard, and making him work hard in return. The massage of his upper body was his reward, for there, he could feel her touch and although he never made comment, she knew that his body responded to the pleasurable sensation that a massage brings.

Her sensitive fingers felt the knotted tensions dispel and, almost daily his leg muscles strengthened.

At other times in the day, she pushed his wheelchair round the garden, making him remember the names of the flowers and shrubs that they identified from a book in his hand.

They did crossword puzzles together, Brett often surprising himself by the answer to a clue. He didn't know when it would come, or where it came from, but it was there.

Other times, Sophie got him into Kathleen's car since her own was too small and she took him on rides through the beautiful Yorkshire Dales and out to Scarborough and Whitby. Though he protested at first, hating to be the object of pity as people watched him struggling to get out of the car and into his wheelchair, he grew immune to their glances.

Kathleen and John were delighted with the small steps of progress that Sophie was making with Brett and returned to their family business with lighter hearts, assuring Sophie that she could have whatever she thought necessary for Brett's welfare, including their presence whenever she thought it needful.

'We're not running out on you.'

Kathleen smiled.

'But it's such a relief to be able to go to work with an easy mind. I have arranged with Mrs Cunningham to see to all the meals and housework, so you only have Brett to see to.'

'That's no problem.'

Sophie smiled back.

'I know Brett's not going to suddenly become the perfect patient, but I think I have the measure of him, and I can give as good as I get.'

One day, Sophie announced brightly to Brett that they were going swimming.

'Oh, no, think again. I'm not taking

that wheelchair for a dip!'

'You'll do as you're told, and like it!' Sophie retorted.

'And how will I get changed? Unless, of course, you care to come into the male changing room?'

He grinned wickedly at the thought.

'No problem. I have telephoned the pool, and there will be someone on hand to assist you! It will do you good.'

And it did. Once Brett was in the water, he felt exhilarated by the sense of freedom. Sophie made him do some of his leg exercises and, though he groaned in mock displeasure, he knew that it was beneficial. He was beginning to feel almost human again and was regaining his sense of self-worth.

Summer rolled on.

Their routine was set, though with variations. Their friendship grew and although deep in Sophie's heart she longed for a return to their budding romance, she deliberately held back, still fearing to lose him when his complete memory returned, as she was convinced it would.

Brett, too, seemed content with their friendship as it was. Although there were times when she found his glance disturbing, as if he were struggling to recall what had been there in the past, when she returned his gaze, the look would flicker away gradually, leaving only a vague smile or a wry grin in its place.

Then, one day, it all began to change.

Sophie was pummelling the muscles of Brett's thigh, using the edges of her hands to drum up and down. His eyes were closed, a serene expression on his face.

Suddenly, she stopped and almost leaped backwards. Brett opened his eyes, looking startled.

'What's the matter?'

'You just winced! You must have felt something!'

'I didn't!'

'Yes, you did. I saw it!'

Sophie's eyes narrowed slightly. She hadn't been mistaken. Without taking her eyes from his face, she sharply ran her nail down his lower leg, until now quite numb to her touch.

'Ouch!' he exclaimed.

'Got you!'

Her cry of triumph faded on her lips.

'Oh, Brett, it's wonderful news! Why didn't you want us to know?'

She was troubled by his denial. Didn't he want to get better, or, for some reason, not want them to know?

Brett sighed and pushed himself up into a sitting position. He held out his hand to her.

'Come here, Sophie. Let me explain.'

'This had better be good,' she said.

She moved up towards the head of the massage table and stood looking down at him silently.

'Don't look like that, Sophie,' he pleaded. 'I didn't mean to deceive anyone. It's just that, well, there has been a slightly tingling sensation for a few days now, but it wasn't continual and I was afraid that it wouldn't be permanent.'

He reached out impassionately.

'Don't tell Mum and Dad yet, please. I don't want to build up their hopes only to have them come tumbling down again.'

Sophie caught her breath.

'Oh, Brett, but it really is a good sign. It is! Really!'

The intensity of his expression, the hope, the fear, the doubt, all tore at her heart. But somehow she had to help him believe in the possibilities that this had generated.

'But, your mother, Brett, she needs to know!'

'Not yet!'

She stared down at him, trying to sort out, not only his conflicting emotions, but also her own feelings. She understood, partly. No! It was more than that. Yes! It must be demoralising to feel that everyone was clinging to a faint hope and you were the one who kept letting them down — thinking it was coming right, then finding it wasn't.

'All right,' she said slowly. 'I'll go along with it for a couple of days, but you just think on, Brett Ridgeway. We've got this far and we are not going back. We're going all out for it. Understood?'

Brett grinned.

'Yes, ma'am!' he groaned, 'but what have I let myself in for?'

10

The next few days were tense for Brett. Every tingle in his toes sent a thrill of hope spiralling round his body. The muscle power in his legs was strengthening with every massage and exercise session. It had taken all of Sophie's strength not to step backwards when he pushed his foot against her that afternoon.

'It's coming!'

She looked exultant, her shining eyes telling him more than she realised. His heart did a double flip. She was beautiful, and his for the asking, he knew.

He had hung back from declaring his growing love for her out of masculine pride, though he knew she would have taken him on gladly. He had thought of the years ahead and had dreaded being a burden to her.

How could he have tied her to a cripple for the rest of her life?

He wanted to enfold her in his arms; to nestle his face into her hair; feel the softness of her skin; and receive her gentle caresses, not from the impersonal masseuse, but as his sweetheart, lover, wife. So why did he still keep a tight rein on his heart?

There was some vague memory taunting him, but every time his mind reached out to take hold of it, it fluttered away and hovered just out of reach.

The memory, such as it was, filled him with an inexplicable sadness, a devastation as great as the loss of the use of his legs had caused, or was he confusing the two issues, transferring the pain of one to the other? Why couldn't he remember?

Sophie looked at him in alarm as his thoughts distracted him so much.

'Brett? You've gone quiet. Is something wrong?'

'It's nothing! A ghost walking over my grave.'

'I hate that expression!'

'So do I. It just seemed appropriate.'

She grasped hold of his hands.

'You're not still afraid that you'll regress, are you? I'm sure you won't. You're building up steadily. I think it's time to tell your parents the good news, don't you?'

She looked earnestly into his eyes. Ashamed of his lack of trust towards her, he glanced away.

'Yes, you're probably right.'

His voice was listless. He knew he was disappointing her. When he looked back again, he could see the light dying out of her eyes. He had hurt her, and, whatever his doubts and fears about her, he couldn't bear to hurt her.

He wanted to protect her, make her laugh, not cry. With an effort, he pushed his doubts away.

'All right, let's have a celebration!' he said as jovially as he could 'And isn't that new exercise machine and tread-mill due today? I'll ring the delivery firm and chase them up, and we'll order a bottle of champagne. The number is in the phone book.'

He thumped his fist down on the massage table.

'There I go again. How do I know that?'

Was that a flicker of alarm in Sophie's eyes? What was she scared of? Was she hiding something? He lowered his eyes, not wanting her to see the light of suspicion.

If only he could remember everything, he was sure there would be a simple explanation.

Whilst Brett busied himself on the phone, Sophie set up a table in Brett's suite of rooms with glasses ready for the champagne. What else? Flowers! Just the thing! There were so many in the garden. Which should she choose?

'Roses,' Brett advised when she mentioned it to him as he came off the phone. 'Mum loves roses. So do I, as a matter of fact.'

Suddenly a flashback of a bunch of

beautiful red roses in his hands startled him.

'Red roses,' he said in surprise.

'Pardon?' Sophie said in obvious alarm.

'Red roses.'

His voice was flat. It was something to do with red roses, that taunting memory that seemed determined to haunt him.

'Yes, all right,' Sophie said and turned away quickly, scurrying down the elevated decking and heading for the rose garden.

Brett had intended to go with her but he stayed and watched her. What was it? What was missing from his memory? He frowned. It was something to do with being in hospital. Had she brought him some red roses? He couldn't remember, though he was sure she hadn't. It was earlier than that, before his accident, not after it. He was giving them to someone, thrusting them at her, telling her to take them. It was an elderly lady — his gran! That's who it was, but why the pain in his heart? The pain hadn't been caused by Gran — it was Sophie!

But, why? What had she done?

He couldn't bear it, the not knowing. It might only be something small, but he didn't know. If it was left unresolved, it might spring into life at any moment, and tear away their present happiness. He had to know! Maybe Gran held the key to it. She was there in the faint memory, he was sure of that!

With a determined clamping together of his lips, he swung his wheelchair around and went back into the house.

★ ★ ★

Sophie snipped the long stems of the choicest red roses that were still in bud, lost in troubled thought. In spite of the warm sunshine, she shivered. Fate was about to strike — she just knew it. All this talk about roses, red roses in particular — had Brett remembered that he had called her his red rose girl?

Or, worse, had he remembered why he hadn't wanted to see her again?

She bit her lip in uncertainty. Was it too late to confess all? But, what could she say?

'I don't think you wanted to see me again, but I don't know why.'

She shook her head. That was no good. No, she would have to wait and hope for the best.

Brett was nowhere to be seen when she returned to the house, her arms full of red roses. She found a large rose bowl with a stem holder inside it and arranged the roses to her satisfaction.

The doorbell rang, announcing the delivery of the two exercise machines.

'Will you bring them in here, that's right,' she told the delivery men.

Where was Brett? What was keeping him?

The champagne arrived next and it would soon be time for John's and Kathleen's return home from work. Mrs Cunningham had left everything prepared for their evening meal before she finished at two o'clock so there was nothing to do, except have a shower and change for dinner. The door to Brett's suite opened behind her.

'There you . . . '

The words of greeting died on her lips, as Brett paused in the doorway. His face held a mixture of sadness and something she couldn't quite determine, something stronger. Was it anger?

What had happened?

'Brett? Are you all right? Is anything wrong?' she asked, a worried frown creasing her forehead.

'You tell me.'

'I don't understand. What's happened?'

'I've been talking to Gran on the phone. She had some interesting things to tell me.'

'Oh?'

She felt a sudden alarm.

'About me?'

'Yes, and your fiancé,' he burst out angrily.

'Fiancé?' Sophie exclaimed in genuine surprise. 'But I haven't got a fiancé.'

'That's not what Gran tells me.'

'Well, she's mistaken! I ought to know!'

'Does the name Robert mean anything to you?'

'Robert? Robert Williams?'

'How many Roberts are there in your life?'

'Don't be sarcastic. It doesn't become you.'

'No, I'm sorry. I'm just finding things rather difficult to understand.'

'So am I!'

She was suddenly concerned about him. She hadn't dealt with any cases of loss of memory and didn't know how rational or irrational such cases were during partial recovery.

'Are you all right, Brett? You look . . .'

'What? Hurt? Blind? Stupid?'

He passed a hand across his face.

'I think it might be best if you just go back to your boyfriend, back to the house he has just bought for you.'

Sophie felt the blood drain from her face.

'This is getting ridiculous. I don't know what you're talking about. I haven't got a boyfriend, nor a fiancé, and Robert was certainly never that. We finished soon after I met you.'

'So, you do admit you were two-timing the pair of us?'

'Yes, well, no.'

She stared at him, her mind paralysed in confusion. What on earth was he talking about?

Her mind suddenly caught up with the rest of his sentence. Robert? Buying a house? For her? Why would he want to do that? As for two-timing either of them! She shook her head.

'I didn't two-time either of you. It was already over between me and Robert, all bar the shouting.'

'It's a pity you didn't tell him so. He seems to be still under the impression that you are to marry him in the none-too-distant future! I'm supposed to be the one with memory loss, not you.'

She flushed angrily. This was getting beyond a joke.

'I haven't seen Robert for ages!' she declared. 'Not since . . . '

She stopped. Not since she had seen him in the reception area of Willowbank Court, and then there were the flowers in Mrs Carter's room, and Mrs Carter's strange behaviour over his reason for being there, some secret she said Sophie would find out soon.

Warning bells were beginning to ring. Robert was behind all of this. What was he up to?

Brett was still watching her face. Had he seen her sudden apprehension written there? His eyes were suddenly filled with contempt.

'What's your game? Softening up an old lady? Trying for a cheaper price? Well, you've got the house now! You've no reason to stay,' he said bitterly.

'What has Robert done?'

'You expect me to believe you don't know?'

'I don't! And I never will, if you don't tell me!'

Brett was still looking at her in disbelief.

'As recently as two weeks ago, he exchanged contracts with my gran. He's bought her cottage, as a wedding gift for you! So, what's your story now? Do you still say you knew nothing about it?'

Sophie was dumbfounded. What nonsense!

'But we'd finished. I thought he was just as thankful it was over as I was!' she tried to explain.

'Then why would he still go ahead and buy the house? He must have had some hope, mustn't he?'

She shook her head.

'This still doesn't make sense, but . . . '

Maybe it wasn't as ridiculous as she had thought. Her mind was slowly making connections. She felt as though an icy hand had gripped her heart.

Robert Williams had a lot of explaining to do!

And what of Brett? She suddenly felt angry. Angry at Robert, for whatever shady dealings he had done; angry at Brett, for being so ready to believe the worst of her; angry at herself for being so easily caught in the middle of it all.

It took all of her self-control not to turn and run away. She wanted to. She needed time on her own to sort through all the turmoil of conflicting emotions that were tumbling over in her mind. She felt caught in a whirlpool, and, swirling around her were Brett, Mrs Carter and Robert Williams! That he was at the centre of it all was no longer a doubt.

Her professionalism as a nurse came to her aid. There was no way she could leave her patient unattended, and whatever Brett might think of her, he was still that, her patient.

John and Kathleen would be home soon and she saw no reason why their delight at Brett's progress should be put in jeopardy. They would go ahead with their earlier plan.

'Right, Brett Ridgeway! You just listen to me! I don't know where your gran has got hold of all the nonsense you have just told me, and right now, I don't care. But I do care about your parents, and they will be coming through that door at any minute and you are going to put on the act of your life. You can be happy, doubtful, hopeful, whatever you wish with regards to your progress, but we will celebrate! You will smile, even if it kills you, understand? And, tomorrow, I will take some well-deserved leave! Got that?'

11

And they did it! Maybe they weren't quite so hale and hearty as they might have been but John and Kathleen didn't seem to notice. They were too overjoyed by what they saw.

Most of Brett's leg muscle wastage had been restored and, to prove his growing strength, he pushed against his father's shoulder with his feet, a triumphant grin lighting up his face.

Together, they got him positioned at the treadmill and he took his first tentative steps. His forehead glistened with sweat and Sophie was sure that the delighted smile he gave her was genuine.

Though she smiled back, her heart was sad. Would he want her, even if she could unravel the tangle of wrong information he had about her? He wasn't trusting her. Surely he would, if he really cared.

She left mid-morning the following day.

It was Saturday and John and Kathleen were at home over the week-end. They didn't ask any awkward questions about where she was going and gladly took over Brett's treatment for the two days Sophie had asked for.

She reminded them how to do the massages, still an important part of Brett's recovery treatment and showed them how to use the exercise equipment. Once the morning session was over, she tidied up and went.

'Have a nice weekend,' Kathleen called. 'You deserve it.'

Sophie did her best to look cheerful.

'Thanks. I'll . . . er . . . see you on Sunday.'

Once in her car, Sophie let the cheerful mask slip. Her overnight thinking hadn't brought her any further enlightenment, apart from strengthening her conviction that Robert was the cause of all the trouble.

Heading south, she turned over in her mind where to go first. She was tempted to hunt down Robert and tear right into him, demanding to know what it was all about. But, on reflection, she realised that would put her at a distinct disadvantage. Robert could be very condescending when he chose and she felt vulnerable enough as it was, without risking being at the mercy of his superiority.

No, Mrs Carter was the place to start.

* * *

'Eeh, come in, love,' Mrs Carter welcomed her. 'Well, I was only talking about you yesterday with our Brett. Kathleen tells me you're doing a grand job with him, and you spending all this time away from that young man of yours, with a wedding to plan. It's right good of you.'

'That's precisely what I have come to

talk about, Mrs Carter,' Sophie said gently as she sat down beside her old patient and began to try to find out what was going on concerning Robert.

And as the pieces of the puzzle began to fit together, Sophie became more and more furious.

How dare Robert go around telling people they were getting married? Why? What did he hope to gain from it? And he hadn't wasted much time!

He'd gone to visit Mrs Carter in hospital one afternoon, only three days after she been taken in there, eager to tell her that he and Sophie were soon to be married. Surely he wasn't still carrying a torch for her? Not possible.

He had made it clear he wasn't interested in marriage, unless it furthered his political aspirations. Was he getting his own back on her, then, for dumping him? No, not even Robert would stoop so low — or would he? And why buy Mrs Carter's cottage? He'd said himself that it was only fit for pulling down!

'Don't be ridiculous, Sophie! I may have implied that we were more than good friends but . . . ' Robert spluttered when she confronted him.

'You told Mrs Carter we were engaged, for heaven's sake! About to be married!'

'Well, so I had hoped, my dear.'

'No! You're the one with that idea! And remember, all of this happened two days after you had walked away saying that you were glad to be rid of me!'

'Mere words, my dear. I knew you wouldn't take them seriously!' he said trying to sound genuinely concerned.

'Well, I did! And you made no move to come back to find out! So, why were you so keen to split up Brett and me?'

'Don't be silly! I don't care whom you set your cap at, or whatever it is you do these days. This Brett fellow is welcome to you!'

'Then what's it all about? Knowing

you, there has to be a reason. And why buy her cottage? What on earth are you going to do with it? I can't quite see you as a cottage dweller, with or without modern conveniences,' Sophie prodded away, determined to get the whole business cleared up once and for all.

Robert adjusted the knot of his tie nervously. He looked particularly uncomfortable.

'Well, if you must know, I saw the chance of making a profitable deal and, well, it was slightly . . . er . . . irregular, if you know what I mean!' he spluttered.

Sophie gaped at him.

'Go on, then.'

'I am relying on you not to say anything to anyone,' he cautioned. 'And I mean no-one! People talk!'

He glared at her for a moment, before continuing.

'Well, you see, there's a new road planned to be going through there, a motorway link road. There will be a large roundabout in front of the Beehive Hotel. The land down the western side of Alexandra Road, where Mrs Carter's cottage is, will be at a premium in a few months.'

Sophie was aghast at his audacity and underhandedness.

'So you decided to cheat an old lady out of some money she was entitled to! How despicable can you get! Didn't you think that she might need any extra money due to her, to see her comfortably through the rest of her days?'

Robert flushed at her scathing tone.

'The old dear's all right. It wasn't a bad price I offered, and her daughter's pretty rich, from all accounts, but you'll know all about that, of course, since you obviously have hopes in that direction!'

Sophie gasped.

'I couldn't care less about John's and Kathleen's financial state, but I wouldn't like to be in your shoes when someone connects your name with your job, and realises that you used inside information. I don't think that will do your career any good, or your political aspirations!'

Robert made a dismissive gesture.

'My name isn't connected to it. Yes, I know Mrs Carter thinks I've bought it but I haven't. I knew she would let me have first refusal if she thought it was for you, and let it go at a reasonable price. And don't look at me like that, little Miss Innocent. Don't pretend you've never played the system.'

He nudged her arm.

'I'll scratch your back, if you scratch mine! Nudge, nudge! Wink, wink!' he said.

Sophie was genuinely shocked.

'Don't paint everyone in your own colours, Robert. I think you've behaved despicably. Who was it for then? Someone useful to your career, no doubt! No, not your career! It's to do with politics, isn't it? You were greasing someone's palm, I think the expression is.'

She suddenly remembered the man

she had seen with him at Willowbank Court.

'Hardman . . . no . . . Hardacre! That's who! Isn't it?'

She could see that she was right.

'Well, I hope you aren't disappointed, Robert, but it's not the way I would choose to progress.'

Robert flushed again under her gaze.

'There's no record that I had anything to do with it, so you'll get nowhere if you try to make anything of it,' he warned.

'Now, why am I not surprised! Anyway, I wouldn't stoop so low as to try! What I particularly don't like about all of this, Robert, is that you have not only abused your own professional position, but that you've also abused mine, by using my position as a nurse to get to an old lady and, in turn, abused her trust. Well, I hope you sleep well at nights!'

She thankfully took her leave and drove home to her flat, still wrapped in the cloying cloak of Robert's deceit, lies and betrayal. A bracing shower made her feel slightly better but she felt restless and kept finding herself roaming around her living-room, adjusting ornaments and plumping up cushions.

Tomorrow, she would have to decide what to do about going back to face Brett with the true facts.

Sunday morning dawned clear and sunny. Sophie wished she suited it in mood. She hadn't slept too well and still hadn't decided what to do. She now knew all the relevant facts but found it difficult to face up to driving back to Yorkshire to explain it all to Brett. He hadn't trusted her, hadn't believed her.

Surely, if he loved her, he would have trusted her. Maybe he didn't love her. After all, he had never actually said he did. Had she read the wrong signals? She would feel such a fool. On the other hand, what did he really know about her? Even if his memory returned completely, he had only really known her for two days before his accident, plus any snippets of information he might have gleaned from his grandmother. It wasn't a strong basis on which to place unconditional trust, was it? Maybe now, after she had explained Robert's duplicity, they could start afresh.

She showered and dressed and went to church. The service helped to calm her fears, and enabled her to realise that, if her love for Brett was worth anything at all, it was worth making the return trip to set the record straight, and to take it from there!

The door-bell startled her shortly after her return to the flat. It was unusual for unexpected visitors to call on a Sunday, and who knew that she was here? Robert! Oh, dear! What did he want? She had nothing else to say to him.

She pressed the intercom button.
'Yes?'
'Miss Draycott?'
'Yes.'
'Interflora!'

'Oh! For me? Are you sure?'

'Positive!'

'Oh, hang on then. I'll come down.'

She ran lightly down the stairs. If this was a bribe from Robert for her to keep quiet about his dodgy dealings with the cottage, he could take a running jump! She'd stuff them straight in the bin!

She opened the door.

'Oh!' she exclaimed.

The most enormous bouquet of beautiful roses filled the whole of her vision. Red roses! She couldn't see who was holding them, until he lowered the bouquet and peeped bright-eyed over them.

'Brett! But how did you get here?'

She didn't really want to know how. He was here, and that was all that mattered. Her doubts about his lack of trust vanished into the air.

'Oh, Brett. They're lovely!'

'Am I forgiven, Sophie? I've come to take you home. I've realised that I don't care what's gone on in the past. I only know I love you and want the chance to start all over again and I hate to hurry you up, but I can't stand here like this for very much longer!'

'Oh, Brett. I don't even know how you are managing to stand there at all! Yes, of course I'll come home with you. I love you, too,' she exclaimed in such excited happiness.

'You do?' he replied.

'Yes.'

They stood grinning delightedly at each other, until Sophie remembered to ask how he had got here!

'Dad brought me. He's round the corner with my wheelchair. Dad! You can come out now!'

A little sheepishly, John appeared with the wheelchair and Brett thankfully let them help him to lower himself into it.

'Kathleen's with Gran. If you haven't had lunch, we rather hoped you might like to come and have it with us,' John invited. 'I'm sure you can tell us somewhere nice to go.'

Sophie and Brett were still smiling

happily at each other. She longed to be able to throw her arms around him and be kissed to death, but they had all the time in the world for that! Brett pulled out one of the roses and held it out towards her.

'A red rose, for my red rose girl.'

Sophie took hold of it and leaned down to kiss him.

★   ★   ★

A few months later, the official plans for the lay-out of the new motorway link-road were published in the local Press. Although the lower end of Alexandra Road was to be blocked off, making it into a cul-de-sac, the proposed lay-out of the link-road was a hundred yards or so to the west. It meant the demolition of the butcher's shop and house and a short row of terraced houses on Chorley New Road but none of the properties at the top end of Alexandra Road were affected!

The link-road passed by the rear end

of their gardens and many house-holders dismally predicted that the value of their houses and land would, in consequence, fall. What a disappointment for Robert and his cronies who had all hoped to make such a financial kill!

But Sophie and Brett weren't concerned — they were too busy planning their wedding.

THE END